Everything Is Broken

Everything Is Broken

Short stories

From

Friday Night Writers

Edited by

John Dufresne

MIDTOWN
PUBLISHING
™

New York, New York

Published by MidTown Publishing Inc.
1001 Avenue of Americas
12th Floor
New York, NY 10018

Library of Congress Control Number: 2013955547

ISBN 978-1-62677-005-8
ISBN 978-1-62677-004-1 (e-book)

Contents

Introduction

By John Dufresne

FRIDAY NIGHT WRITERS

Three of the four students from my Fall 1989 Poetic Techniques class wanted to keep meeting after the semester ended. We set up a Sunday afternoon session at my rented house in the shadow of I-95 in Hallandale. We met sporadically through the semester, sometimes with only two students attending. The house was inconveniently too far north for some. So I decided to move the sessions to FIU and to hold them on Friday nights. That way, I figured, only people who really wanted to write would show up.

We gathered in the breezeway on the second floor of AC2. We sat on benches at picnic tables. We did this for a few years. We complained about the mosquitoes, the feral cats, the squirrels climbing the concrete walls around us, and the occasional foraging raccoon, but we kept meeting. When the weather didn't cooperate at all, when the rain blew sideways through the breezeway, we retreated to the nearest open classroom. Eventually, I wrangled a room just off the breezeway. At some point the acoustics got so bad, we couldn't hear each other. That's when we hit on the idea of AC 2 110 as our classroom—a well-lighted amphitheater. And we've been there ever since.

Hundreds of writers have come through the group over the years. Some stay for a short while; others have been with the group almost since the beginning. Steve Almond was writing for *Miami New Times*. He attended during the breezeways era and was writing stories about Russian peasants. He's now the author of seven acclaimed books of fiction and nonfiction and is a commentator on Boston's NPR station. The late, great Barbara Parker brought several of her novels to the group when the books were in their early stages—we were her first readers. She wrote twelve novels before her untimely death a few years ago. Preston Allen's stories of church boys and other sinners first appeared at our Friday night sessions. I could go on.

What is this Friday night writers group anyway? Let's start with what it is not. It's not a social club or a mutual admiration society. It is not a debating society. It's not a repair shop. It is not a fight club or a soapbox. We're not here to expound on our ideologies or to defend a particular theory of literary criticism. We are not literary critics, after all, not while we're in AC2 110 at any rate; we are creative writers. Critics, in the words of Kenneth Tynan, know the way, but they can't drive the car. We want to be behind the wheel, not whining in the back seat. We want to invent the highway. (And with this automotive conceit in mind, E. L. Doctorow said this about fiction writing: "It's like driving a car at night. You can't see further than your headlights, but you can make the whole trip that way.") The group might be described as a family, albeit, a dysfunctional one. We think of it as Thanksgiving dinner every other week with a few creative works of fiction, nonfiction, poetry, and screenwriting as the main course.

It is a place to have a conversation about a creative work. Not about a writer. About the work on the table for discussion. A conversation, not a series of pronouncements. And it's a conversation that flows, that is give and take. Ideally, the conversation flows organically, comments follow comments; you amend another reader's observation or disagree with it, or you jump in with a new suggestion, idea, question. One thing leads to another. We don't interrupt. We listen to each other. A conversation, then, followed by a deep breath.

The readers converse; the writer listens and takes notes. Each of us brings to the conversation our own aesthetic principles, our own tastes, our own past experiences, our own expectations, writing and reading histories, and so on. And so this means that there will be disagreements about the work in question. And none of these disagreements needs to be settled. As a writer you can and should expect to hear conflicting responses to your story. Writing a story, you understand, is not done by consensus. We're here simply to help the writer make the work the best it can be. We do that by responding with generosity, honesty, specificity, and humility. And as writers we take what we can use and we disregard what does not make sense. Our most important relationship in the Friday night group is with our work.

You have in your hands an anthology of short stories, *Everything Is Broken,* our first publishing venture. The stories were chosen from the Friday night writers' submissions during our summer break. We wish we could have chosen more, but we're starting out modestly. The stories here document the way we live our days now, very often alone and in dire straits. The stories were chosen for their beguiling voices, their vivid sense of places, their compelling and intriguing characters, their tension, and their suspense. These are stories about what keeps us up at night. Important stories. The subjects are as splendid as they are varied: a talented young swimmer longs for a family and for love as he swims against his arch-rival; a young grocery worker/rock guitarist finds himself lured into a fundamentalist church by a— what else?—beautiful woman; two lonely souls drift through the city streets hoping for intimacy and settling for diversion; a group of old friends, retired firefighters, honor a dead colleague, a suicide, and face the extermination of their own dreams; the quirky wife of a rising political star suffers a breakdown on the eve of the gubernatorial election; an athletically gifted high school student escapes her wealthy adoptive parents in search of the life, the culture, and the family she was taken from.

Thanks for picking up this book and reading it. We're all apprentices here at the Friday Night Writers; we're all practicing our craft, making up brave new worlds, and telling each other stories of the many goodly creatures who live in them.

Everything Is Broken

Fervor

By
Michael Creeden

Pat went to jail in February of '86, thus ending our band and what remained of my musical career. I picked up more hours at the supermarket and tried to figure out what the hell I was going to do with my life.

Food Mart was not the best place for a slightly depressed ex-musician to work. It was a low-end supermarket in southeastern Massachusetts. They bought off-brand groceries, cheap cuts of meat, and overripe produce the better markets wouldn't touch. Their motto was "We Stack it High, We Sell it Low." If you bought produce on the day it came in and you ate fast, you could get some real deals. But the stuff spoiled quickly, so in the mornings before the store opened, we *pulled* the garbage: going through the counters, pulling off the overripe fruits and vegetables and dumping them into a shopping cart. After we spread what remained on the counters so the place looked slightly better than the day after Armagedon, we retired to the back room to *do* the garbage: picking through the cart to find the still edible produce, which we bagged up and loaded onto the reduced rack. You could get a bag of bruised apples for sixty-nine cents, a couple heads of iceberg lettuce, stripped of the green outer leaves and left with the whitish core, for forty-nine. In Fall River in 1986, those were some good deals. Tuesdays were the worst. The weekend shopping depleted the shelves, and produce delivery was scheduled for noon but was always late. And I had to work with Ron Rego, who liked to talk.

"You have to have a reason to get up in the morning." He grabbed a bruised Golden Delicious and opened a new plastic bag and dropped the apple in. "Something that drives you." He delicately pulled a squishy tomato from the pile and dropped it into the empty barrel behind him, where it landed with a splat.

"Otherwise you wind up like the people that shop here."

"Pat had drive," I said. "Look where it got him. Jail."

"Harrington was pretty good singer but he was no Bruce Dickinson." He dropped a handful of moldy chestnuts onto the metal cutting table. They fell—*clack, clack, clack*—like poker chips. Who the hell bought chestnuts?

"Iron Maiden being the gold standard of musical excellence."

"Harrington wasn't willing to pay his dues. You don't bust a guy's elbow with baseball bat just because you think it's your turn. Or your buddy's turn." He gave me his "I'm-crushed-by-your-human weakness" Vince Lombardi stare. When he was washed up in about two years, Rego would make a hell of a peewee football coach.

"You don't cheat fate. You wait it out. Look at me: eleven years I been waiting."

Rego was almost thirty. He'd been a part-timer in produce since he was nineteen when he walked away from a full football scholarship at the University of Rhode Island because he couldn't stand going to class. He didn't think it was fair that you had to go to college to play in the NFL; they should have minor leagues like they do in baseball. Finally his patience was being rewarded: a couple of towns away on I-195, New Bedford was starting a semi-pro football team. Rego was training for the tryouts in a couple months, in late July.

He looked at me, waited. This was the part where I was supposed to say: "You're right, Ronnie. I'm too talented a musician to sit on the sidelines bagging rotten fruits and vegetables. I need to rock," but the fact was, I wasn't sure I did. One thing I was sure of: I needed to get away from this guy right now.

Bananas were always fresh because they came in every day. I looked at the boxes by the door and decided we needed some out in the aisle.

"I'm gonna put up some bananas." I pulled off the stained smock—it was like a big lab coat for people who operated on rotting fruit carcasses—and threw it on the cutting table.

Rego hocked a lunger and spit it in the barrel.

"Don't milk it. Truck will be here any minute."

I threw two boxes onto my cart. Before I pushed through the plastic dividing strips between back room from sales area, I peeked through them to check the scenery.

"Any talent?"

The aisle was empty except for a thin woman picking through the remains of the lettuce. She looked vaguely familiar, but she was dressed very conservatively. Her long denim skirt and pullover sweater were a strange fit for early summer in New England.

"Just some old librarian type," I said, and stepped out onto the floor.

Despite the warning, I milked it. I was tired of doing garbage, tired of Rego's inspirational speeches. I loaded and re-loaded the bananas twice. First time I went straight up and down, then I went diagonal left to right. I had pulled them off to go right to left diagonal when I got a meaty fist in my lower back.

"Last time," I said. "Just give me a second."

He leaned over and whispered in my ear. "You know her."

"Huh?"

"The chick in the *Little House on the Prairie* outfit—you know her."

I shrugged. I didn't know her.

"She used to go to Olympus. She used to be hot. She used to be a *twag*."

A twag was a medium-hot older girl who worked it all the time: high heels at the beach, makeup in the supermarket, hoopy earrings in the gym. The woman in the aisle was definitely not a twag, but I turned to check anyway, peering over Rego's beefy shoulder.

It was Donna Davis. She had been a regular at Olympus where I used to DJ. She used to be a party girl. I had almost gone out with her about ten times. Now she was…not a twag. She looked toward us. I panicked and ducked.

"Get up!" He slapped me on the head. "She's gonna think you're blowing me."

I grabbed two overripe bananas from the garbage box under my cart. "No I'm not," I said, handing him one. "I'm getting us a snack."

Rego peeled his banana and bit half off and started chewing.

"She's probably a Jehovah now." He dropped the peel in the box and shook his head. "It's a freaking waste. Why do they have to take all hot chicks? Some of these Jehovah deals are loaded with hotties. I don't understand it. They're gonna dress them like that why don't they take the fatties? Leave the hot chicks for us heathens."

Donna moved across the aisle to what was left of the salad items. She glanced over at us while she fingered tomatoes. I couldn't tell if she recognized me, resplendent as I was in my produce department vestments.

Rego slapped me on the shoulder. "If you're gonna give your life to Jesus, make it quick. You need to unload that produce truck soon."

I waited till Rego disappeared, then wheeled up the opposite side of the aisle. I stopped in front of the acorn squash, roughly across from Donna. I watched her in the mirror, checked her cart for signs of weirdness, like arugula or soy products, but it was just normal food like Cocoa Pebbles and hamburg buns and regular milk. She still hadn't noticed me. If she'd been twagged-out, I would have considered stopping by to say hello. I pushed my cart toward the back.

"Kenny! Hey! I didn't know you worked here."

I always felt embarrassed when people said that. I was a twenty-five-year-old community college graduate in a depressed mill town. Did people expect me to work at the UN?

Donna wheeled her cart over. She was smiling, which was different. She'd always done the moody/smoldering/depressive thing. I liked it. I thought it showed sophistication. I found her disposition the most attractive part of her, after her shoes. She always wore sexy shoes. Now she was smiling and not wearing sexy shoes. In fact, she was wearing the most unsexy shoes ever made: those little flat white sneakers that looked like they'd been shipped in from 1958.

"You didn't recognize me," Donna said, prompting.

It was true. Besides the clothes, there was something weird

with her face—it was like she'd gotten surgery to make her plainer.

Rego was right. I saw the whole script unfolding in front of me. I was supposed to say, 'Hey, you look different." And then she would say, "I'm not a moderately attractive and heathen twag anymore. Jesus has changed my life and he can change yours." And then I would reach into my jacket for my box cutter and slice open my carotid.

But of course none of that happened. What happened was, I jumbled my lines.

"Donna. Hey, how's it going on?"

She smiled, and I took it as the sign that she wanted me to lean over and give her the Hollywood cheek kiss that she always wanted people to do when greeting her.

Apparently that had changed. Donna leaned back as if to avert a speeding bus. Then she recovered and held out her hand and gave me a firm shake. We stood there awkwardly until she got tired of waiting for me to ask.

"I'm a Christian now. I go to the new church on South Main, the Temple of Christ."

I nodded. There were a few non-Catholic churches in Fall River, but they didn't tend to do so well, what with Massachusetts being well-educated and, oh, about a thousand miles north of the Bible Belt. I stared at her small eyes, her thin pale lips and it hit me: no makeup.

"It's made a huge difference in my life."

I could see that, but I wasn't sure it was a difference worth making. But then it took me about ninety seconds to find a way to see Donna as sexier in her holy elusiveness. More sexy than all those nights at Olympus when she let it all hang out, when she'd go out with any yahoo with muscles and work boots. I was trying to think of something to say when Rego peeked his head though the strips and said, "Truck."

"It was nice seeing you, Donna, but I have to get back to work."

"One sec." She reached into the baby seat and opened her purse and pulled out a card. "If you'd like to come to church, we'd love to have you Sunday morning."

She rushed through, but she got her lines right. Just to be

polite I glanced at the card. The church's name was in the foreground, a ridiculously beautiful family in back—husband, wife, and three daughters, the older two around my age. Interesting.

"Pretty, aren't they? The church has a band, too."

Oh God, I could just imagine. Stryper was big then, the Christian hair metal band. I pictured the preacher dressed in black and yellow spandex tights, whipping Bibles into the crowd as flash pots exploded on stage.

But then our eyes met and I saw a flash of the old Donna, slightly trashy and delicately fucked-up. She smiled. "You're different, Kenny. I've always known that. You should come."

What else did I have going on?

It was like what you see on TV, only it seems crazier when you're actually there: people ran the aisles and shouted and sang and yelled gibberish and danced around as if they were possessed. The band didn't wear spandex, but they did sort of rock even though the bass player lagged and the songs had that slightly sickening "I love Jesus" aftertaste. Donna sat a few rows in front of me, and she really seemed into it; she rolled her shoulders and grooved her hips in a way that seemed a bit sexy for church. She was dressed more like her old self too, in a clingy, out-clubbing dress that, judging from the conservative dresses on the other women, would soon be retired if she remained Pentecostal.

For the first ten minutes of service the band vamped on a chorus of "Jesus on the inside, working on the outside." The guitarist sang in a thin, reedy voice that was more like a warble. Every two minutes he looked toward the unoccupied pulpit with the black Les Paul guitar beside it. It was like the Revue waiting for James Brown.

Finally, the preacher came out. He was a big dude, broad in the shoulders like an athlete and sort of All-American good-looking, albeit with a certain mileage on his face. He strapped on the guitar and immediately fell into rhythm with the band, then started belting the chorus in a deep baritone voice. He strutted around like he was born onstage, smiling at the congregation and the band and playing little country licks between verses. The crowd went nuts.

His name was Jack Moody. A year earlier, he and his family, along with about a dozen other people from their church in Forth Worth, Texas, had moved to Massachusetts to establish the church. It was a musical family: the preacher's wife, a silent woman known only as Sister Moody, played keyboards, and his youngest and oldest daughters, Jenna and Mira, came up to sing with the band. Mira, the oldest daughter, was around my age. She'd graduated from some Bible college in Delaware and was awaiting an assignment to her own church. The middle sister, Leanne, was twenty-two, and young Jenna was eighteen going on twelve. When Mira and Jenna got up to sing with the band, Leanne remained seated in the front row, living up to her surname.

The preacher led the band through a couple of original songs, most of them variations on a theme: *I thought I was a star until I screwed up my life, but then Jesus came along and made me a superstar*—the under-utilized Jesus-as-impresario motif. You could see how something like this would be popular with poor Fall River people who were going nowhere, and the energy of it did made me miss being in a band, but I wasn't buying the rest. I never would have come back if Donna hadn't invited me to lunch with her and the Moody girls.

We went to Sagres, a Portuguese restaurant on Columbia Street in the south end. In the year they'd been in town, the Texans had apparently fallen in love with spicy Portuguese food to the point where this lunch had become an after-church tradition. Donna and I picked the appetizers: Shrimp Mozambique in a spicy, red, garlic sauce, and a couple orders of spicy grilled chourico. While we made small talk with the Moodys, who asked us about Fall River and Portuguese people, I looked at Donna for signs that she was interested in me. Since she'd come in to the store and invited me to church, I'd been thinking about the possibility of us getting together—not so much because I really wanted her, but, honestly, because it would have been something to do. On the way to lunch, I'd concocted a scenario in my head: lunch was about the Moodys screening me as a potential boyfriend for Donna.

That theory was quickly smashed by Donna's constant questions about "guitar man," who I assumed the dorky backup singer in the church band. It was somewhat appalling, if only for the fact that I was a better guitarist at eleven than that guy was. But I understood the attraction: he was from someplace that was not Fall River.

I hadn't been paying much attention to the Moody girls at all when the youngest, Jenna, started raving about the food.

"Sister Donna, this food is *so* good," Jenna said as she dipped a crust of Portuguese bread into the garlicky Mozambique sauce. "I didn't know you were Portuguese … are you?"

Donna, deeply engrossed in the carnal pleasures of Portuguese food, must have forgotten the sanctified company she was keeping.

"Only by injection."

Mira, the oldest, stirred her diet soda and tried not to register a response, Leanne smirked, and stupid little sheltered Jenna blundered on, "What do you mean?"

Donna speared her shrimp and swished it around in the sauce and said, "Seven inches of hot chourico, that's what I mean."

Leanne cackled, then looked at me and smiled. Mira took a deep breath and closed her eyes, probably said a silent prayer to Jesus. Jenna finally got it, and her gasp resurrected Sister Donna.

"Oh my god, Oh my god, I'm sorry. I'm so sorry." Donna's head moved from side to side, as if she were trying to rewind the moment. "I don't know what got into me."

"Probably Satan," Jenna said. "Ma says that it can take a long while for sinner girls to change. But Jesus is patient."

Donna looked like she wanted to punch Jenna, but her eyes shifted pleadingly at Mira. "Do I have to get baptized again?"

Mira smiled gently. "No, honey. Don't worry. I know it just slipped."

Leanne snorted. "Everybody needs a slip every now and then."

"Leanne Elizabeth Moody," Mira said. "Stop it now."

The slip comment, and the way I thought Leanne looked at me when she said it, kept me coming every Sunday for the next month. They had coffee and donuts in the back room after church—fellowship, they called it—and I tried to engage Leanne whenever I could. She was my kind of girl: moody loner, on the outskirts of things. She was much more attractive to me than Mira, her more conventionally-beautiful sister. Mira seemed destined to marry some famous Pentecostal preacher and become Tammy Faye to his Jim.

But the church had strict rules about dating and sex. Christians were only to date Christians, and then only as a brief precursor to marriage, which was, coincidentally, the only time they were allowed to have sex. This explained why church people married early. It also explained, to me anyway, why Donna had gotten baptized after only her second service: she was interested in making herself available to "guitar boy" (aka, Luke the Warbling Welder).

The Moody girls had a small problem though: the only church people at the Temple of Christ were the ones who had moved up from Texas to help start the church. Most of them, outside of Luke, were married. They needed to convert people, and fast. The other alternative was to meet people at revivals: preachers would travel around the country preaching at various congregations. That was how Jack Moody met his wife Linda, it was how Jim Bakker met Tammy; and, I feared, it might be how Leanne would meet her future husband.

Jack Moody announced it during my second service: the church would host its first revival at the end of the month, a big-shot preacher from Wisconsin was coming to preach and save souls. Supposedly, he had three handsome sons, one or two of whom were around Leanne's age. I felt like I had to press harder with Leanne. The first couple of times I asked her out, on the Sundays immediately following the Seven Inches of Hot Chourico luncheon, she'd laughed, as if I'd just told a bad joke then said in a southern drawl she could put on at will, "I think I hear my momma callin'." Then she'd smirk or wink and then walk away. A few times when I was working Leanne in some corner of the fellowship hall, I'd see Jack Moody, looking at me and watching. I tried to read his face but I couldn't.

Then after one service—two weeks before the revival—Mira and Jenna had again gotten up to do a special with the band. It would have been easy to think that Leanne simply wasn't musical, but for some reason I knew that wasn't true.

Leanne was talking to some new converts, older Portuguese grandmother types (vavoas), when I walked into the fellowship hall. I waited a minute, then suddenly lost my enthusiasm for my weekly trip on the flirty road to nowhere. I turned to walk away.

Jack Moody stood by the door, surveying his flock. He caught my eye. Then he looked over to where Leanne was ending her conversation. Then he looked back at me.

Was Jack Moody telling me to go flirt with his daughter?

I walked over, said hey. Leanne dragged *hi* out to three syllables, looking over my shoulder.

"Is he watching?" I asked. She nodded. "Why?"

"I think he likes you," she said. "I have no idea why." She didn't break a smile.

"Maybe it's because he can see that I'm a charming, hardscrabble young man who's on his way to great things in this life."

She did her little snort. "Yeah that's it. Either that, or Donna told him you were a musician. Among other things she told him. My Dad likes musicians, obviously."

"What kind of other things?"

"Umm, I'm not sure but maybe she told him that you were in this band with this loser named Pat, who was kind of a sleazy big-talker type who one night when you were all at a bar attacked some guitar player with a baseball bat so you could get into a band?" She smiled straight at me, showing her snaggletooth. "Maybe it was that, but I'm not totally sure. I got it from Jenna and you know how she is with all that Satan business." She wrinkled her face into a thoughtful look.

"So essentially, I think my father sees you as one of those follower types: follow a bad guy, become a bad guy, follow a good guy, become a good guy."

"I'm not a follower." I looked around the room, made a grand sweep with my arm. "Nobody to follow here. I'm here under my own free will."

She nodded. "Impressive."

"Can I ask you a question now?

"I don't know. Can you?"

I really wanted to ask, are you really into all this Jesus business, but given this was our first actual conversation, I thought I'd better hold off. Instead I said, "How come you're the only member of the amazing Moody family who doesn't sing? Not into music?" Based on her personality, I figured she was deeply into something, though, maybe poetry or painting.

She looked around. The crowd was starting to thin. The Sagres lunch thing had stopped once Donna started seeing Luke the Welder. They went off alone after church every week, doing whatever welders did at lunch. I don't know why I was jealous—I didn't really want to be with Donna anyway. I probably resented the mileage Luke was getting out of being from elsewhere.

Leanne nodded across the room, toward the poster map of Worldwide Missions.

"Come over here. I want to show you something."

We stood in front of the map. Leanne's finger swept toward the bottom of Africa. There was a little face push-pinned to South Africa.

"Do you know what this is?"

"A dork." A dork named Brother Roger Dalgety, according to the caption. That was the name of the family coming in from Wisconsin, to revive the sinners of Fall River.

"Correct." The smirk felt like a kiss. "I dated him in high school. He was kind of cool then. Now look at him." My heart leapt at this hint of rebellion and sourness in Leanne. "I find most Christian music cheesy as all get out." She leaned against the map. "If I do something, even here, I want it to rock."

I tried to sound casual, but my mind was on fire with thoughts of my playing James Honeyman-Scott to Leanne's Chrissie Hynde. "I can probably help you with that," I said.

When Pat and I had the band, we rented a practice space in an old office building in downtown Fall River. Renting practice space was cheaper than renting an apartment, so when I moved out on my father, I stayed at the office. It was two big rooms: the larger one had probably once housed a secretarial pool back in the day, but we'd carpeted it from floor to ceiling to sound proof it. When Pat went off the rails, I changed the lock so he wouldn't try to hock the equipment, so we still had amps, drums, and microphones, everything. The smaller room, which I imagined had once been some boss's office, had my couch, my stereo, and an old desk that doubled as my dining room table. I slept in a sleeping bag on the floor.

Leanne knocked at the door at five the next night, a Monday. She was supposed to be out door-knocking, but she'd faked sick. She was dressed kind of sexy for a Pentecostal girl: short jean skirt, white blouse with two buttons open, a bit of jewelry, and combat boots. The boots hit me as trying a bit too hard, but she looked good in them. Her hair was in that partly up and partly not kind of thing with the little tendrils framing her face. When she hugged me hello, I smelled perfume.

"This place is awesome," she said. "I can't believe that people still have offices down here. What do they do?"

"Insurance, bail bonds, there's an eye doctor on the second floor, but he's about ten thousand years old. And there's this rock and roll emporium on the third floor. It's a real Tin Pan Alley."

Leanne had a notebook, a brand new one with the song written on the first page, lyrics with chords written over it. She looked at me looking at the book and said, "I copied from my other notebook. There was other stuff in there I didn't want you to see."

For the next two weeks, Leanne came over Monday, Tuesday, and Thursday night to work on her song. It was coming along. When I wrote, I'd always found the lyric-writing to be sort of embarrassing and corny. Most people don't notice what rock lyrics are saying, but I still had a hard time putting anything down on paper, so I was glad that Leanne took that part. The words weren't bad, and they were exactly what I would expect from Leanne, sort of a jilted lover's note to God, about how he didn't understand her. At least I thought it was to God. She wrote it in a way that you could take it both ways. Real crossover appeal. Freed from the embarrassment of writing, I got into creating riffs and chord progressions like I had ten minutes to live. I hardly ever got calls, but for some reason, the phone was ringing off the hook. My machine was broken, and after I while, I just unplugged the phone.

Wednesday was church, which she could not skip. With my new inspiration, I even went the Wednesday night Bible Study.

It was a little more serious than the Sunday morning hootenannies: less music, less fiery preaching from Jack, more Bible analysis. But at least I could look at the back of Leanne's head. I wasn't bold enough just yet to sit with her. I would have sat with Donna, actually, but she wasn't there.

The Friday before the revival, I went into Food Mart at ten A.M. for the long, hellish Friday shift. The place would be mobbed all day, right up until closing at nine P.M. On Sunday, I would play live music for the first time in almost a year. Yeah, it would be in front of a cheesy church audience, but I guessed it was better than nothing. I hadn't told Rego about the whole thing, but I figured I would. He'd probably laugh, but part of him would be happy, I thought, so what the hell. I slapped through the plastic dividers and burst into the back room.

"Heh-lo, Mr. Rego. What the fug is going on?"

He had a watermelon laid on out the table, had the machete-like cutting knife over his head when I burst in. He winced and shook his head. I'd apparently broken his concentration. I waited as he realigned the melon then raised the knife over head and brought it down. The melon split open with a crack. Perfect cut: not a seed in sight. He quickly sliced the halves into quarters and moved them over to the table between cutting and wrapping. I grabbed one and put it on the wrapper while Rego lined up his next victim.

"What's up, stud? How's it going with you and the Jesus girl?"

I told him it was going OK, we were working on music, and that we were going to have an actual date the next day, the Saturday before the revival.

"She's gonna put out? Whoa! Shocker. Is that why you dumped Donna for her?"

"I didn't dump Donna. I wasn't even *seeing* Donna."

"Reeeaalllly? Now that's interesting." He hacked into another melon then stopped so I could catch up. While I wrapped, he cut a slice from a melon and started gnawing on it.

"I been seeing Donna at the Belmont every night this week, shit-faced and crying in her fucking Rumplemintz about some guy. I assumed it was you."

The Belmont was a bar downtown. It tried to be better than the average Fall River bar, but it was really just the same as all the other bars, which is to say seedy and somewhat depressing, but with couches, arm chairs, and coffee tables scattered about.

"Donna was drinking?" She'd been borderline alcoholic since I'd known her, which was one of the reasons why I thought church was good for her. Church people were strict teetotalers.

"I'm not sure I'd call what she was doing drinking. I'd call it getting hammered."

"You're not lying are you?" I assumed that something happened between her and the welder. He broke up with her or got called into the mission field. Or maybe he was just an asshole.

He snorted. "I'm gonna make something up, I'll make a better story than that up."

When my shift ended at nine, I called Donna but she didn't answer. I stopped home to change my shirt and got to the Belmont at ten. The place wasn't that busy yet; people tended to hit the Belmont last, so they could pass out on the couches. I spotted Donna at the bar, loaded and wearing one of her sexier church dresses. An old construction worker type wobbled toward her. I cut him off and shook my head. "My sister's had enough for tonight, sorry."

The guy held up his hands apologetically and took one last look at Donna before stumbling away. I slid into the seat next to her.

"What are you tryna do?" she slurred. "He coulda been my next boyfriend."

"They're not your people, come on. What's going on? I wanted to call you when I didn't see you in church Wednesday but my phone's been busted."

Donna pounded her beer chaser and looked up at the ceiling and slapped her hand on the bar. She had a ring on her thumb, which reminded me of Pat's saying: girls who wore thumb rings were sexually adventurous.

"You went to church Wednesday? Oh that's great. How's Leanne? Are you gonna get baptized so she'll let you kiss her?"

I shrugged. The whole thing started hitting me in a weird way. I called the bartender over and ordered a beer. Donna wanted another double, but I talked her into just a beer.

"My buddy said you've been here every night this week. I thought you were sober."

"Sober-drunk, saved-sinning, what's the difference? I'm still the same fuckin' loser I was the day I was born."

If I was in some movie, I would have had a snappy comeback, but the fact was I'd had been having the same conversation with myself at least once a week since 8th grade.

"Maybe there is no difference. But at least you weren't hurting yourself."

She frowned at me. "Putting yourself in danger, I mean."

"No?" The bartender put our drinks down. Donna looked at him. He waited but she shook her head. "Maybe later." She took a long drink of beer. "Why are you coming after me now? When you were at Olympus doing your DJ thing you never noticed me." Which wasn't actually true. I had noticed her and contemplated asking her out a bunch of times, but Pat always bashed her.

"Actually, I did notice you. But I always forgot to put my muscles on and tuck my tight jeans into my work boots before I left the house, so *you* never noticed *me*."

Donna flipped me the bird and smiled. She had long, sexy fingers, and they were painted black. "Tou-fucking-ché. Smart ass. So what am I gonna do now?"

The old construction guy was eyeing us from across the bar, probably waiting for me to screw my move so he could slide in. I glared at him. He shook his head, went back to his beer.

My beer looked like a prop in front of me, so I picked it up and drank half of it.

"You know what sucks?" she said. "You know what really sucks? I liked it. I liked going to church. It made me feel good. Like I belonged somewhere."

"So keep going. What's to stop you? You felt like you didn't fit in?"

"A guy happened. What else?" She smeared the booze puddle in front of her. "Fit in. That's a nice choice of words." She looked at the bartender, then at me. "It's only been five. I was barely starting when you got here."

I doubted that, but I nodded anyway. Who the hell was I to say?

Donna raised two fingers and the bartender moved to the tap. Donna looked at me. "I might not have fit in, but Luke tried to fit in…to my snatch."

"Are you saying he tried to rape you?"

She shook her head vigorously. "No. No, of course not. He wanted to do it, though, which is OK, but it's the *attitude* he had about it. Like I was just gonna give it up because of who I used to be. And who he was. Big church man."

The bartender had brought our shots. For some reason, I felt inclined to pick hers up and hand it to her. She took it and smiled and said cheers. We clicked glasses.

"I don't expect you to understand this but: if Luke was a scumbag and tried to get at me, it probably wouldn't have bothered me as much. I would have expected it. But he's a virgin. He's twenty-seven years old, and he's never done it before."

"He wanted you to teach him?"

"Yeah, I guess." She slid her beer right under her, stared at the foamy top. "You know what he said, though, it's so fucking weird. He said, "Fuck me like the whore of Babylon.""

She looked at me and her eyes looked suddenly very clear.

"Those people are so fucking weird," I said. We burst out laughing.

On Saturday, Leanne and I were supposed to do a few last run-throughs of the song at the office, then we had to go to church and practice the song with the band. When she rang the downstairs buzzer, I had half a fleeting notion to tell her she was a hypocrite and a liar and a crazy church bitch, that the world wasn't created in seven calendar days and that there was in fact a thing called evolution, that she and her whole fucking family had ascended from apes just like the rest of us heathens. I wanted to tell her to fuck off and leave me alone and get Luke the Welder to write a song with her.

But I didn't. I couldn't. She didn't like Luke any more than I did—she had in fact warned me about him, had told me to tell Donna that he was a little off and not to be trusted, especially where women were concerned. But I didn't say anything. I didn't say anything because having Donna hooked up with Luke left me free to go after Leanne. And what had happened, happened.

And then Leanne was knocking at the old wooden door of the office. When I opened the door, I could tell by the way she was dressed, in a really short skirt and a tank top and her hair down and all crazy and licentious-looking like only Pentecostal hair can look, and perfume and the boots, that she didn't intend to spend the whole time working on the song. The day before the revival, too. These people really have a flair for the dramatic, I thought. And when we were on the floor of the office, rolling around on that old maroon rug that was full of cigarette holes and coffee stains and had decades of Fall River dirt and misery pounded into it, as I rooted in and out of Leanne, the words of that chorus came into my head: Jesus on the inside, working on the outside. I almost said it out loud but I didn't want to ruin the moment.

I got to the church early on Sunday. I wanted to get my amp sound perfect for what might be my one and only performance in the United Pentecostal Church. I'd told Donna that night when I brought her home about me and Leanne and the special that we were going to do at the revival. I begged her to come. Said it would be like Olympia, only funnier. Instead of a drunken George Kousoulas grabbing the mike and yelling at all the Fall River losers to cash their welfare checks and dance and buy some drinks, Brother Hot Dalgety Dog would tell them to dump it into the offering plate and dance and come kneel and give their lives to Jesus.

When I pulled into the parking lot, Jack Moody's van was already there, along with some beat-up Datsun. No one was in the church when I walked in, but the pastor's office was closed. I heard muffled voices behind the door, but I couldn't make anything out. I went onstage and did set my volume a little higher than was needed, and my tone a little dirtier. I played a few riffs. Part of me felt bad about making noise, part of me wanted Jack Moody to hear. I got into it and kinda lost myself, so I was a bit surprised when I heard the clapping behind me. I turned around.

It was Luke. "Sounds great," he said in his stupid accent. "I didn't know you was a player."

I didn't know you was a player either, you douche. And then I figured he might not know I was friends with Donna and why get into it with him today. He was probably out back, carrying on as usual, making plans for his next street preaching gig or whatever the hell else he did. He would be there when Donna and I were long gone, so what was the point? I nodded and said thanks. Jack Moody had stepped out of the office and was watching us from the back wall. For a charismatic guy, Jack Moody did a lot of watching from corners.

"I look forward to hearing your special," Luke said. "You're the first person's ever gotten Leanne to perform publicly. Pastor Moody says she's phenomenal, but we've never heard her. I can't wait." Luke raised his hands. "Well, I oughta get cleaned up for service. Tell me your name again?" I told him and he said, "See you soon, Kenny."

Jack Moody waited for him to leave before he approached the altar. I was kneeling and putting my guitar in the case, so we were at eye level.

"Luke told me what happened between him and Sister Donna." He looked down. "It's terrible. Luke should know better. He's been in the church all his life."

I snapped my case shut. "Yeah well," I said, trying to approximate a Texas drawl, "just a sinner gal. Prolly lot more where she came from."

I expected him to be pissed, but Jack didn't take the bait. He shook his head. "Prolly not, my friend. I've had some conversations with Donna. I bet there's not a hell of a lot like her, even in this town."

I climbed off the altar and slid my case off. I looked up at Jack, shrugged. He put his hand on my shoulder. "I'm glad you're still going to do your special. You would be totally justified if you chose not to because of what happened to Donna, but I'm thankful that you're going through with it. It means a lot to Leanne."

I nodded. "It's a good song she wrote. People should hear it."

When I arrived at ten-thirty the parking lot was packed. In the six weeks I'd been coming I'd never seen the lot more than half full. In all that had happened over the past two weeks—Leanne, Donna, Luke, the song, and my return to playing in front of a crowd—I'd completely forgotten about the focus of the revival: a big shot revival preacher was coming to town with his wife and his handsome sons. The whole Dalgety clan sat in the front row left: the wife, with the classic long flowing Pentecostal hair, the two moderately good looking sons, and a young daughter of about eleven who seemed to have of some of Leanne's snarky alienation about her. I liked the kid immediately. While the band warmed up the crowd with the usual choruses, Douglas Dalgety sat on a metal folding chair at stage right next to Jack Moody. When Jack stepped out to do his thing, Brother Dalgety watched intently. I got the feeling Jack was intentionally lying low, like a kickass opening band trying not to upstage the headliner.

I figured I'd go all out that day, so I sat with Leanne in the third row right, in the exact same seat where Donna had been sitting the first time I visited. Leanne had a similar blouse to the one she'd been wearing at our first rehearsal, a black skirt, black tights, and the boots. A few of the old Texan ladies wrinkled their noses when they saw Leanne, but she didn't care. I kept looking around, waiting, hoping Donna would show up and slide into the aisle seat I'd saved for her, but by the time the choruses ended and the songs started, she was nowhere to be seen.

Specials typically came just before the preaching. So after the choruses, Jack Moody put down his guitar and stepped to the pulpit with a huge smile on his face. He was finally going to get to introduce his daughter, who I now understood was the most talented of his talented family. Suddenly, Brother Dalgety stage-whispered "Pastor."

Jack went over and talked to Dalgety, who apparently requested we do the special after preaching. I thought he was worried about being upstaged, but he was the guest of honor. After the altar call, the song could be almost anti-climactic. Leanne didn't seem to mind; in fact, she whispered, it would be better, as the song would be the last thing people heard that day.

So Dalgety went first. He wasn't all that, but I could see

why people liked him: he was a big stew of raw feeling seasoned with vocal vibrato. His main move, which he used at least three times, was to tell a sad story about someone's fall into sin, voice getting softer and sadder as he went, only to whip around at the end with a loud, obnoxiously vibrated *oh*, *but I want you to know tonight!* It was like watching a three A.M. infomercial. Jack Moody, on the other hand, was more like a teacher than a preacher, and he had cred with me because he had done things outside the church. If I'd come in during the ministry of Dalgety, I wouldn't have lasted five minutes, no matter how sexy his daughters were. But if one were a Christian and prone to believing in weird little signs, one might have taken note of the texts with which he begin his sermon.

Dalgety pulled his Bible out from under the pulpit with a theatrical flourish. "I'm to speak to you fine people today about *fervor*. Turn in your Bibles with me this morning to the book of Colossians, chapter four, verse twelve." He looked up, waited for the few people in attendance who had Bibles to open them. Leanne had a small pocket Bible, which she opened and held up for us to read. Her attitude was changed a bit. She seemed more serious. It wasn't the first time she'd had sex, but she hadn't been tearing it up either.

"The Lord is speaking through Paul, and he says this:

Ephrasus, who is one of you, a servant of Christ, saluteth you, always laboring fervently for you in prayers, that ye may stand perfect and complete in all the will of God."

Leanne pinched her lips together in a tight smile. I wondered what she was thinking. Did she feel bad? Did she not care? Dalgety was talking again.

"And then we are going to go to Acts eighteen and twenty-five. And it says this:

This man was instructed in the way of the Lord; and being fervent in the spirit, he spake and taught diligently the things of the Lord, knowing only the baptism of John."

His sermon had a few interesting tidbits, but most of them drowned by his overuse of vocal pyrotechnics. I kept thinking about the song, anyway. I was suddenly afraid I would botch something, that I would forget the chords, or have a case of digital

Alzheimer's like I had during the sound check before our biggest gig ever, Toad's Place, in New Haven, Connecticut.

After he finished, Dalgety did the altar call. A couple of *vavaos* went up there and knelt at the altar, along with this wiry guy I'd seen around town, at the library, walking down South Main; occasionally he'd come into Food Mart and buy a bag of reduced apples off the discount rack. He was exactly the kind of sad guy I would expect to be responding to altar call, but whatever, if that's what he wanted, let him have it. And then it was time for us to go up there.

Jack Moody went to the pulpit in the post-altar call swelter and whispered into the microphone, "We have one more thing for you tonight. Leanne and Kenny have a special."

As we'd practiced it, the song was an uptempto riffy blues tune, like early Creedence Clearwater. It seemed weird to perform a tune like that at the moment, so as we walked up the aisle, I leaned over to Leanne and said, "What do you think about doing it a little slower?"

She looked at me and nodded. "Of course. How else would we do it?"

The band fell into time perfectly, even Luke and the lagging bass player. I played guitar and Leanne sang and quiet Sister Moody's eyes welled up while she played the hell out of her piano. The best part was midway through, when I looked out over that weird church crowd and saw Donna sitting in back, alone, smiling her sad smile and nodding to the music with everyone else.

Semper Fi

By
Ingrid López

The driver keeps glancing over his shoulder, like he needs to check that Usmari hasn't disappeared. She's never asked him to drive this far into the ghettos of New York City, to stray so far from the itinerary The Boss assigned. Thirty-three minutes ago, Usmari walked off the locker room at Van Cortlandt Park with two hours to game time. When the door closed behind her, when the latch bolt clicked into the strike plate with that heavy metallic thump of fire doors, she walked out on the most important meet of the season.

Usmari noticed the blip this morning. She's always queasy the day of a big match but this feeling was different. It made her think of a sonar ping getting closer. Its presence pulled her away from classes, from lunch, from the hour she spends in the language lab learning Punjabi to talk to her Sikh driver in his native tongue. By noon, the weight of two years in her Upper East Side Petri dish had started to weigh her down with an unshakable physical presence.

At 3:17p.m., the very moment the Town Car turned left at W 165th Street and edged the side of New York Presbyterian, the eerie, unexplainable pressure eased by a degree.

"This is good," she says, a few blocks later and taps Gurinder's shoulder. She reaches for her book bag. "Stop right here."

Gurinder double parks beside an idling minivan. The driver shoots him a stare of death and Gurinder replies with a few choice words in Punjabi. In the back seat, rooting through the front pocket of her book bag, Usmari tries to decide what to take. Cash, of course, and the credit card she liberated from The Boss' pocketbook two nights ago. She tucks a wad a twenties into her right tennis shoe.

"Do you need pick up, Miss?"

"I'll call," Usmari says. She waves her phone and gives him a cautious smile.

Usmari can tell he has wanted to challenge her decision since she got in the car, but he also wants to keep his job. Live-in driving gigs like his are few and far between. Usmari may only be Carol and Prescott Locbs' foster kid, but unless they pull rank, Gurinder is still a driver and Usmari is the flat-chested fifteen-year-old who can boss him around. She turns off her cell phone and slips it in her pocket.

She gets out of the car, slams the door, and looks both ways before crossing Broadway. She waits for the little man to flash on the crosswalk signal and makes a dutiful stop in the median until the Town Car merges into traffic. Gurinder's blue turban becomes a little dot and then disappears in the glare of the windshield.

Usmari has this tugging feeling, like the corner should be familiar. The street sign says she's on Broadway and W 164th Street. There's a coffee shop in front and a pharmacy behind her, but the landmarks look all wrong. She sits on the little bench and tries to picture the corner way back in oh-three. She takes in the smell of exhaust and coffee and *rabo encendido* from the Dominican restaurant that took over the bail bonds place.

There's a new bodega too, across the street, where the check cashing place used to get robbed twice a week until the owner took to sitting by the door with a towel on his lap and a twelve-gauge loaded right under the towel. Only it's not a bodega anymore. Now it's Pereyra Supermarket, with blue awnings, rusty ice coolers, and windows chock-full of posters for beer and calling cards. Usmari zips up her warm-up jacket. Her Brearley track uniform looks a bit less conspicuous this way. She's sweating almost immediately.

She crosses the second half of Broadway and dips into Pereyra to get out of the heat. She lingers at the door to let her eyes adjust to the darkness. The cashier looks bored in his little nook near the entrance, prostrate on his Plexiglas altar. The bins behind him are packed with bodega cash crops: lollipops, cold pills and cigarettes.

Bowl-shaped mirrors are perched above the shelves at strategic angles. The signs between the aisles are misspelled. Usmari moves through cramped rows of canned food, past the miasma of nearly spoiled apples and a box of cucumbers dripping something white and disgusting, like vegetable pus.

She takes a full minute to scan the bodega and wonders where she fits now, if there's a place for her amidst the pockmarks of what used to be her life. She doesn't smell like too sweet perfume anymore. She doesn't wear braces or clunky glasses from the Gift of Sight do-gooders. Carol and Prescott Loeb—yeah that one, the hedge fund star—have invested in contact lenses and Invisalign retainers.

Usmari takes diction classes, French classes, art classes, boxing classes, and birth control to keep her face pimple-free. She's gone from long, spindly legs and nappy curls to a mirage of her former self: well trained, well fed, and scrubbed free of any evidence that points to her birthplace. She needs to shed this prissy, Upper East Side persona and embrace the girl she used to be: Usmari Consuelo Trujillo, from Washington Heights.

She stands behind a tower of Tampax boxes covered in filmy dust. From her vantage point she can follow the cashier on a mirror and keep an eye on the door. Her watch beeps. It'll be three more hours before Tía Jessenia gets home from Pet Haven Crematory where she shovels dog ashes from the ovens into porcelain urns in the shape of fire hydrants. Tía Jessenia lives only an hour from the Loebs' brownstone, but Usmari has visited once in two years. They met outside a McDonald's by Central Park.

Usmari tries to imagine Tía Jessenia's face when she comes home from work and finds her sitting on the stoop, tells herself Jessenia will be happy to see her, not pissed because Mocho, her live-in-boyfriend would give his left nut to play the wrong kind of daddy with her only niece. She tries to remember why she'd wanted this life so much, and it comes to her with the ding of a bell and the bodega door opening in. A girl comes in. She's clad in short-shorts and a tank top, wearing pink Timberland boots. She looks rough around the edges, ghetto pretty—like

Usmari before skin treatments and five-hour Keratin blowouts. In the Heights, her hair, her skin color, the lilt to her speech will give Usmari the thing she misses most: anonymity.

Here neglect is immediate. Tía Jessenia won't give a shit about her, just like she never has, just like the Loebs, but at least she'll be honest about her apathy, won't pawn off childrearing on a bevy of schools and a full staff.

Her mouth waters at the thought of a world where she's not a perpetual beacon of awkwardness among perfect-smooth girls with names like Greta and Matilda. This world will be happy if she doesn't get pregnant before eleventh grade. Here Carol Loeb's friends won't look at her like a sideshow freak, jealous of the upstart socialite from Jersey, of the wily ways she used to land a hedge fund manager *after* he made his money, to insinuate herself into all the right boards and committees, whose kid goes to the Brearley School even though she's five and still wearing diapers.

Usmari wonders if Carol knew Brearley would never take the pale, cumbersome lump she was able to wrestle from her womb before it dried up for good. She had to. Most parents could never think that of their own kid, but Carol is a shrew. She knows her kid underperformed across the board. She knows her kid got dealt a heaping bowl of idiot and not an ounce of savant. And none of it fazed her. Carol didn't sit at home, bemoaning her substandard offspring.

Carol got moving. Carol scouted he best sprinter in five boroughs—and an underserved minority to boot—and sold her to the Brearley School as a package deal: bragging rights and a star athlete and Lower School admission for Tinsley Loeb, no questions asked. It's like that story about Mary and the Virgin Birth, the kind of shit you can only pull off one time. Once again, Usmari will breathe easily. She won't be paraded like a show horse, expected to serve as proof of her foster family's boundless altruism.

The hot mamacita slinks down the aisle with the baby formula and returns a minute later with a can of Nestlé Good Start in her hand. Usmari waits for the cashier's attention to land on the hot mamacita's ass. The girl is young and shapely. She has her hair up in rollers, big and plastic, wrapped in a rayon bandana with a busy print like a poor man's Pucci scarf. That's the thing about the Upper East Side. Two weeks north of Fifty-Ninth Street and you'll never mistake rayon and silk.

Mamacita looks familiar to Usmari, but she can't quite see why. She moves slowly, dragging out her strut, pushing the baby carriage. The gold hoops in her ears catch glimpses of the overhead light. The earrings have the mamacita's name spelled out in flowery cursive script, *Jennifer*, crossing each hoop.

Usmari gawks because the name sounds like it means something, and the answer's in the glinting light. *This* Jennifer and Jennifer Guzmán—the very zenith of Public School 129's social strata, the girl whose Gucci was never from Canal Street—are one and the same. Usmari is awestruck. Jennifer Guzmán was only a year ahead of her in school, so now she can't be older than seventeen, but already, Usmari can see stretch-marks like maps on her hips and baby spit-up cutting paths down her back.

Suddenly, the ne plus ultra of seventh grade looks... uncouth.

Jennifer pays for the formula with a food stamps card and Usmari scrambles to put away the candy she wanted, to shove the Snickers and the Milky Ways in the deep front pockets of her warm-up jacket. She moves into plain view as Jennifer leaves the store. She hates that she wasted such a good distraction, passed up the perfect chance to eat for free. But at least her mind is made up. She's gonna wait for Jessenia.

She takes out Carol's credit card and grabs food from all three food groups: salt, sugar, and soda. At the Loebs, everything has to be nutritious, organic and fat-free. The chef buys produce daily. Cheetos are yellow-cake uranium. The cashier gives her a bored once-over and lines up her snacks. He picks up each item, enters their UPC by the digit, pecking at the register keys with an index finger.

The gothic D tattooed on one of his knuckles looks fuzzy, like his tattoo artist was her little cousin, the retarded one whose mom didn't stop drinking while she was pregnant, so now her kid can never color inside the lines. Usmari stares at the selection of gum and candy under the Plexiglas and points out a pack of Juicy Fruit and three cherry lollipops. She tries to spy the rest of the writing on the cashier's knuckles. Noticing, the man makes fists and bumps them together, flashing the full range of his knuckles. They spell HARDCORE.

"Eight fifty, *mi niña*," he says, and starts bagging Usmari's dinner.

Usmari slides the credit card across the counter. She hears her stomach rumble. Already she can taste salty chips, feel the cherry soda washing down the Cheetos. HARDCORE swipes the card through the reader. The screen comes alive, the word P R O C E S S I N G slides right to left. Usmari bites the nail on her pinky. The screen flashes twice.

D E C L I N E D.

D E C L I N E D.

The cashier fumbles with the bagged junk food. "What's it gonna be? You got cash?"

"Try it again," Usmari says, summoning her best Carol Loeb impression.

HARDCORE doesn't get that he's supposed to do what Usmari wants. Instead, he peers at the credit card intently, taps it on the counter. "It still gonna be expired."

Usmari feels her face getting hot. *Stupid*, she tells herself. The card expired last month.

"Cash," she says, at last. She drops to one knee to get the money in her sock, but keeps her back straight so the candy bars won't slip out.

Two girls come in, like ghosts of her past in Washington Heights. They're wearing the standard uniform for Public School 129 John H. Finley, collared blouses, blue knee-length skirts. They eye Usmari, her hair, and Usmari eyes them. They get in line. HARDCORE makes a *hurry-up* gesture. He rolls the bag on the counter and makes a move like he's going to put everything back. Usmari eyes the door.

The future comes to her in a flash, a glimpse of herself, running down the street, catching the A train to the Upper East Side, munching on the chips, back in her soft, perfumed life. And then the flash is gone because that'll mean facing Carol's wrath. She'll have to explain ducking out of her chance to take home the Mayor's Cup.

She snags the shopping bag.

Soda cans clang against the counter. She swerves past the girls and out the door and the last thing she can hear before she's out on the street is HARDCORE yelling.

"Grab her," he says to no one because no one is going to get involved.

She coils the bag around her wrist and keeps running east, on Broadway, to the subway. She looks over her shoulder right before crossing the street, and that's when she sees HARDCORE in pursuit. She curses and zigzags through the cars in the intersection without waiting for the crosswalk signal. She puts real energy into getting away, game day energy. A part of her is surprised at how easily HARDCORE keeps up.

The soda cans tumble in the shopping bag, crushing the Cheetos. HARDCORE's voice grows louder, yelling at her in staccato Spanish, insults mostly, about her mother, calling the woman names that Usmari can't help but agree with.

The edges blur on everything that's not directly in front of her.

Usmari feels the knowledge coming back, her old self settling in. She recognizes the city at this speed. Shoplifting was her thing. She's rusty, but that's okay. It'll come back. She savors the wave of contentment that washes over her belly, knowing she made the right decision to skip out on the Loebs. She has that feeling like this is her territory, like finally she belongs, and that when HARDCORE's hand grazes her jacket. He's not close enough to grab her, but she pumps her arms faster.

This should be her moment, and now she can't rejoice because HARDCORE is just the sort of idiot who leaves a store unattended to chase eight-fifty worth of sodas and chips. She ducks at the next cross street, avoiding traffic. People glance at them like an afterthought, like she's the Roadrunner and HARDCORE is the Coyote giving chase. She loses track of everything except the obstacle just in front and HARDCORE gaining ground and cursing behind her.

Her lungs burn from sprinting six city blocks, past the subway. This never would have happened to the old Usmari. *Damn it.*

She looks over her shoulder and it delays her enough for HARDCORE to grab her and fling her onto the plastic sandwich board outside the nail place on 171ˢᵗ Street. They slide a good six feet on that board, Usmari trying to get out from under HARDCORE, dragging her forearms and the shopping bag through the sidewalk, glad that she put on her jacket before her little concrete surfing spree.

She starts screaming before HARDCORE can get his bearings.

"Help me!" she yells, taking a big gulp of air. Her side throbs. "I don't know this man!"

People care now that she's amped up the drama. They start taking in the scene, HARDCORE yelling, one hand flailing in the air, the other with a tight hold on her jacket. Two men get involved, and they try to get HARDCORE's attention. Foot traffic clogs the crosswalk in under a minute. A yellow cab honks, but no one reacts so the driver leans on the steering wheel, really lets her rip.

Usmari doesn't stop asking for help, but she doesn't stop gauging the strength of HARDCORE's grip on her clothes or the gap between the Good Samaritans, the gap she can exploit if only she... she thinks it and does it almost simultaneously. She rams the shopping bag with the soda cans into HARDCORE's crotch. He stops moving, stops breathing, and wails, arms flying to cradle his groin. She sneaks past the Good Samaritan, still holding on to the chips and the soda but the second one stops her, all care and concern.

"Are you okay, little girl?" he asks. Usmari looks over her shoulder.

"I called the police," a woman says, grabbing Usmari's wrist. "It's going to be okay now." Her cell phone is still out, still open, and she's holding it like a cowboy holds his six-shooter. She's clad in a frou-frou pantsuit and Nike running shoes.

"Can I call someone for you?" the woman says. Usmari shakes her hand free.

For the next six minutes, Usmari is not sure who says what, only that she's pelted with attention and blocked on every side by people heaping unwanted concern on a moment that wasn't even supposed to happen.

How the hell did HARDCORE manage to catch her?

"Hold on," someone says. Usmari looks at her feet. Noise builds around her, rush hour, construction, the hum of nosy pedestrians who want a glimpse of the hoopla.

"Don't let her go." HARDCORE is slumped on a heap against the wall, breathing hard through his nose, letting out long gasps, rallying. "Bitch took my money!"

The Good Samaritan wants to call Usmari's mom. Usmari wants to call her mom too. She hasn't been to Rikers in six years, since Child Welfare moved her in with Tía Jessenia because her Grandma had gone back to smoking crack.

"Where's her parents?" someone asks.

Two chirps of a siren break up the writhing crowd. Usmari sees a sliver of a police car, white and blue, then the NYPD motto on the back door, *Courtesy Professionalism Respect*. She drops the bag of chips and tries to kick it out of the circle, to shove her way free off these people. The car doors slam and the crowd parts amidst orders to make room.

They ask something and she can't hear the question over her own heartbeat. Someone shoves Usmari in front of the policemen. She digs in her pocket and takes out her cell phone. She hates the sound of the T-Mobile chant, how it mocks her for ending up like this. She can't bring herself to dial.

One of the officers starts taking names and dismissing people. The crowd thins. Usmari looks at the phone, feels tears in her eyes because suddenly she's thinking about her mother. She takes a deep breath and tries to think happy thoughts, think about anything except the inmate information she looked up last week, on the Department of Corrections website, think about anything except the twenty-two years, ten months and twenty-four days before her mother is up for parole.

Usmari knows that at Rikers you get twenty-one minutes of phone time every five hours. She's never talked to her mom on the phone, not once in fifteen years, so that's 229,320 minutes her mother has chosen to refuse her phone time or call someone else.

"Hey, what's your name?" the officer asks. From his tone, Usmari can tell he's repeating himself. His lips are thick, pink, and almost girly. He shakes his head and asks again.

Usmari dials Gurinder's number and hits send. She brings the phone to her ear.

"Stop," the officer says. "What do you think you're doing?" He's almost barking.

She answers, tells him she's giving up, tells him she's gotten soft and stupid, that she wouldn't waste her time calling herself either, but her voice comes out all weird, weak and faltering, and that's when Usmari realizes that she's bawling outright, that her face is full of tears and snot. Defeat tastes like the time she got jumped in fifth grade, like coppery blood pooling in the back of her mouth from where she bit her tongue because a punch caught her unaware. She starts retching.

"Sit down," the officer says.

Usmari looks at the back seat of the patrol car, but he points at the curb with a look on his face that says *forget about throwing up in my ride.* She sits down with her head in her hands and her knees close to her chest.

They take down HARDCORE's statement. Usmari lets her mind wander in and out. She can hear bits and pieces of HARDCORE's tale. People keep passing them on the sidewalk and some of the cars on the street slow down, but they look away quickly. There's no blood and gore. No one is getting beat up. Usmari shoves her hands in her pockets. The candy is still there.

"Miss Usmari," Gurinder says, and Usmari looks up. She's never been happier to see her driver. "I call Carol. She is coming."

Usmari looks at her watch. It's been less than thirty minutes since Gurinder dropped her off, but she feels like half her life is gone now. The street is thick with cars, with taxicabs, and yellow school buses. The only reason he's here is that he never left. Usmari blushes, feels even more inept. Of course he called Carol.

"Are you okay, Miss Usmari?"

She cringes at the sound of her name. How she hates this name, jarring and made up, assigned without ceremony. She wants so badly to give it meaning, to hold on to the story her mother told her the one time she was allowed to see her in a visiting room at Rikers, that she'd been named after the United

States Marines because they stood for courage and honor. She would have given anything to have left right then, to take that story and build her mother's myth around that lie.

But she couldn't. She'd hounded her grandmother for weeks to let her come. The visit was birthday and Christmas. It was getting straight *As* in math and science in two report cards. She'd gone determined to burnish her mother's face in her memory, to remember the curve of her eyebrows and the shape of her face. She'd pledged to ignore the mean things she said and the way she slapped the Plexiglas just to startle her. And now she only remembered how her mother laughed, a mean, high-pitched hoot that went on and on until Usmari started laughing too, wondering if she'd missed the joke. But she didn't and she sat there and listened to her mother tell her to be thankful she hadn't named her Semper Fi.

A Town Car stops across Broadway, on the left lane, beside the median. Cars back up past the intersection. Brakes shriek, horns wail. The driver gets out, indifferent to the noise and the protests, and holds the back passenger door open. Carol emerges from the car, her face half hidden by Audrey Hepburn shades. She takes two dainty steps, like she's crossing a sea of liquefied shit. Prescott Loeb alights behind her.

Even from far away, Usmari can feel their eyes appraising her, their pony.

"What happened?" Carol asks. Her arms are crossed on her chest. Usmari looks Carol up and down, defiant. She's taller by a good four inches. Carol is wearing vintage Chanel and it's only four p.m. Carol doesn't break out the vintage Chanel unless the sky is falling.

Usmari can already picture Mrs. Sainz, her social worker curling her lips, filling out transfer papers to send her to the group home in Queens. She tries to imagine her old life, no allowance, no car service, and sweltering nights on her aunt's couch, head buried under a pillow, trying her best to ignore the sound of Mocho and Tía Jessenia grunting and moaning on the other side of the wall.

And this brings her a moment of sheer, beautiful clarity when she sees the real Carol Loeb, wearing her apathy like a string of pearls, when Usmari allows herself the option of trading on her height and her litheness, of making it the hell out of the Heights like Tía Jessenia said she could.

"I was afraid of letting you down, Mrs. Loeb," Usmari says, in her best little girl voice.

They drag out the moment. Usmari looks at her feet, but she's careful to square her shoulders. Mock surrender is all about balance. She wants to acknowledge Carol as the alpha bitch, but she doesn't want to roll over just yet. HARDCORE, the Loebs, the NYPD, even Usmari and Gurinder get into a circle.

Mr. Loeb makes the first move in his pasty, rich-man way. He starts to apologize, calls the whole thing a misunderstanding. That's the moment Usmari knows she'll be okay. Mr. Loeb pats his jacket and takes out his wallet. HARDCORE can't hide the glint of joy in his eyes as Prescott Loeb folds several crisp hundred-dollar bills and makes his offer. Usmari can feel the change in the air, in the policemen. She sees them switch gears, from enforcers to peace agents. This is one less incident to write up.

Money changes hands.

Maybe she could get into Harvard. They'd eat up an essay like hers. Tía Jessenia told her Harvard is the American Dream, and there is no one better in all the land, no one more qualified to sell the ethos of a nation than she: Usmari Consuelo Trujillo, a real-life Cinderella from Washington Heights.

"Come," Carol says, herding her to the Town Car. "You can't be late for the race."

A Hole in the Night

By
Louis K. Lowy

"**H**e shouldn't have done it."

"Yeah," I say.

"His fifteen-year-old, I heard she saw him do it. Awful," Oscar says.

"It's a goddamn pisser," Tabor says.

"Yeah," I repeat. Someone pushes into me from behind, but it's okay. The church we're standing in, one of those quickly built suburban jobs with deep-colored faux stain glass, white stucco walls, and dense Berber carpet meant to muffle sound, was too small for the line of shoulder-patched white-shirted, and blue-shirted, and black-jacketed firefighters circling outside and around the sidewalk; all the way to the church-owned day care across the lawn. I like that. The brotherhood.

"How was he getting along with the Mrs.?" Oscar asks me.

"As far as I know, okay."

"She saw it too," Tabor says. "Right in the living room."

We come to an oak-stained easel that holds an open, black leather-bound book. I jot my name, as do Oscar and Tabor, on a page framed in printed red-marble that says *Relatives and Friends*. As we continue on, Oscar and I take a gold bookmark-shaped paper lying next to it titled *The Eternal Goodness*.

"I don't get it," Oscar says. "Fifty-one, good health, *retired*, not a care in the world, and he does this to himself and his family? It's doesn't make sense."

"It's a pisser," Tabor says. "How long you been retired, Elmer?"

"Me?" I say. "Six years this August." Tabor has about ten

years on the department. Oscar maybe six. I know because Oscar got on just as I was leaving. I like them both. Tabor because of his traditional principles and just as traditional mustache. It's a brown bushy thing that vines down and frames each side of his broad chin. Oscar because he's young, brash, self-assured; what I imagine I was when I knew more than I really did.

"You ever thought of doing that?" Tabor asks me.

Mostly I like both because they have the heat in their bellies—born firefighters. They're big, barrel-chested, tattooed beefy-armed men, stronger than I ever was. You have to be that way these days to pass the physical. Wiry, flat-chested guys like me, they have a rough time. "Heck, no," I answer.

"His poor kid, she must have seen his fuckin' knife wounds. Rescue said they went all the way through and out his back," Tabor says. "Did himself in while she was studying. I don't get it."

"He musta really wanted to die," Oscar says. "I mean if you gotta do something like that, go into the woods where no one can see you."

"In Miami?" Tabor says.

"Carajo. Then charter a boat and do it in the bay!" Oscar says.

"He was a good fella," I say, more to myself. The other two nod. We approach the honor guards, who hold sentry on each end of the white casket. I recognize one of them, but the other five must have gotten on after I retired. Their starched, timed movements, brass-punctuated epaulettes, white gloves and gold-banded bell caps add dignity. At least that's something his wife and daughter can cling to.

I nod to the guards and approach the open casket. Though I'm not big on it, I look inside. His face, faint and lean, still has the boyish look that never vanishes from people like him—blond hair and smooth skin—even after the blond is sanded with gray and the skin is crumpled around the eyes like the corners of a tucked-in bed sheet. I'm drawn to his thin lips, locked tightly together in a single straight odd formation as if a sculptor has slid her thumbnail from below his one cheek to the other. The straight line corners upward at each end as if the modeler, at the last moment, has decided to push up on the damp clay and give the face an upbeat expression. The peculiar curvature resembles the bottom of a kayak. I can't decide if his kayak smile is a nod to, or a repudiation of, his life. A worthlessness creeps over me, and I want to turn away, but I feel as if he has wrapped his chilled palms down on my thinning hair and locked my skull into place, making me focus on the eerie expression until I can no longer bear it. I force my eyes away and focus on his gold captain's badge, the same as my father's, pinned above his left button-flapped pocket. The metal represents goodness, courage, devotion. I want to remember him for that, but I can't stop imagining him ramming a butcher knife through his gut with such power it penetrated his back and jumped out the other side. *Oscar was right, he really wanted to die.* I don't know why, but I feel ashamed.

"Honestly, Elmer, we don't know," says Luis, a first-rate guy and the current union president. He's tall, about thirty-five. His height and dense premature gray hair are a good fit for a man in his position. We're standing outside along with Oscar and Tabor. Luis is off-duty like the other two, and like all of us, he's dressed in dark slacks and a somber, button-down collared sport shirt.

"Some people can't handle retirement," Luis continues. "They lose their identity. I just don't know."

It's very late afternoon. The sun is washed-out and nearly gone, creating a backlight of red and burnt-orange behind the clouds. The viewing line has diminished, barely peeking outside the church.

"He coached his daughter's softball team," Oscar says. "I'd cut off my left nut to have the time to do that."

"Did he say *anything* to *anyone*?" Tabor asks.

Luis shakes his head. "Nothing you could pin down. The crew said he was alive on the way to the ER and should've pulled through. He screamed a couple times that he didn't want to live and from there he went downhill."

"Lost his will, I guess," Tabor says.

"I remember when East Coast Chemical shot up," I add. "He was a rookie lieutenant, just appointed and a few years before he made captain. I was still on tailboard, studying to take the engineer's test."

"How long ago was that?" Oscar says.

"About twenty years. We were in the middle of breakfast, griddle cakes and coffee, when we got the call. From the station you could see thick smoke tumbling across the sky."

"You guys rode a three-man crew in those days, didn't you?" Tabor said.

"Yeah, I was on tailboard. Big Ron Yerby was the engineer, and like I said, he was rookie lieutenant. We slipped on our bunker gear, and I jumped on the tailboard of old Engine 4, the *American LaFrance*. Yerby, who had a hot foot, charged out of the station, sirens screeching all the way to the warehouse district."

"We don't ride the tailboard anymore," Oscars says.

Luis opens his hand toward Oscar as a signal to not interrupt, so I continue. "It was worse than I thought. Being Sunday, you know how deserted it is there—nothing but buildings, rats and chain-link fences. It had all night to flare up. The heat smacked hard on my ears and cheeks. I lowered my visor and raised my collar. East Coast Chem was an old boxy thing, about three-quarters the size of a football field, with a pair of large overhead doors. Overgrown stinkweed separated the warehouse from its neighbors."

"C.B.S.?" Tabor says.

"Yeah, with a concrete roof," I say. "The structure ripped and snorted like it had whooping cough. And the smell, *Jesus*. Even after I tightened my self-contained, that charred plastic-stink curdled my nostrils and pores for the next few days. Occasionally, a blast like an M80, blew from inside. I'll tell ya, fellas, it was a barn burner."

"You were the only unit on the scene?" Luis says.

"At first. Like I said, he was a rookie lieutenant, so I expected he'd have the heebie-jeebies big time. As he hopped out of the cab, I corner-eyed him, watching him size-up the situation." I lower my head to watch my loafers, but really to watch the burning building in my mind.

"Then what?" Oscar says.

I look back up. "He ordered a reverse double-lay with a hard suction hook-up to the hydrant, which was about a half-block away. He and I pulled the skids from the hose bed, and then the deluge, and damn near everything else our gloved hands could grab. By this time the walls were blistering and the heat had singed the stinkweed.

"Your adrenalin must have been kickin'," Tabor says.

"Like a mule after a bee sting. I hopped back on the tailboard and signaled Yerby, the engineer, to take off for the hook-up. The lieutenant stayed behind. The pumper rolled and the hose snaked out of the bed. We connected to the hydrant, but there was a problem."

"The water flow, right?" Luis says. "The city keeps jerking us around with that."

"No. After we hooked up I heard a long, low grumbling, and then a *bo-boom*! I looked back fast and caught the roof ripping from the walls—a perfect pancake. A giant blue firestorm where the ceiling used to be. My throat caught and I nearly vomited my breakfast cakes. I headed back to the fire in double-time, frankly afraid of what I'd find." I glance at the fellas. They're nodding their heads, as if remembering. I doubt if any of them ever experienced anything like that. *You can train, you can study, you can practice, but in that split second, when there's no thinking, no rationalization, no sarcasm, humor, bullying, bluffing or ego; it all comes down to character. The weaker ones fall back and protect the exposures, the stronger ones step forward and wrestle the fire demon.* I don't know how to convey that to the fellas, or even if I have to. "Damned if this rookie lieutenant hadn't pried open both overhead doors, had the deluge connected and shooting five-hundred gallons per minute over the breeched roof, and was signaling me to help him drag the three-inch nozzle into the darkest, most solid smoke wall I ever saw in my life. He was a good man, a good guy to share sweat with." My skin prickles. It surprises me the jump I get from reliving the story.

"It ain't like that no more. Too many pussies and too many lawsuits," Oscar says.

"You old timers were the real deal," Tabor says.

Luis nods.

I'm fifty-eight, I hate being called an old timer.

"Anybody for drinks? We can catch happy hour," Tabor says.

"Can't. Wife won't let me."

"You're a pussy, Luie," Oscar says.

"Elmer?" Tabor says.

I shrug. "Sure."

"See," Oscar says, "he's not worried about pissin' off his wife. Are you?"

"No," I lie.

"The real deal," Tabor says.

Luis shakes our hands and leaves. The rest of us agree to meet at the Hialeah *Flanigan's*, a chain sports bar not too far from the church.

I enter my silver Avalon and glance at Big Red, Ladder 2, the 105-foot Pierce Aerial Apparatus that's parked across the street in the empty elementary school parking lot. The truck's there because the on-duty crew has stopped by to pay their respects. That's the truck I drove when I was an engineer. Big Red is a grunting, snorting Goliath whose air horn steamrolls man and vehicle aside as it grumbles along. Separate or be crushed. Where does a blazing red, half-a-million dollar, forty-foot long beast park? Anywhere it wants. I feel a sling of desire to blast its horn again as I pull my Toyota from the church pavement.

Grand Turk. I never had a longing to visit the capital city of the Caicos Islands, though I've heard it's nice—one long sugar beach and a marigold sun flickering in the turquoise tide. I'm a city boy, forced transplant, when I was five, Pittsburgh to Miami. Dad was looking for better weather and a clean start. He ended up a firefighter. I ended up a firefighter.

"Here's to the brotherhood." Oscar raises his mug.

I pull my eyes from the colorful Grand Turk map laminated beneath the surface of the blond-wooden bar we're sitting at. Flanigan's is a noisy, lumber heavy, nautical themed bar-and-grill with rows of large TV's imbedded below the rafted ceiling.

"And to the recently departed," Tabor adds.

"Hear, hear!" I toss in. We clack our mugs, swallow, and Tabor adds to them from the beady Heineken pitcher covering his laminated map.

I like hanging with active duty personnel, belly-up to the energy, the youth. Their passion sparks me. I like listening to Oscar and Tabor moan about administration, contract negotiations, escalating runs and lack of man power; essentials that, after you retire, no longer have meaning.

"It was a lot better in your day."

"You think?" I say to Tabor.

"I think it was goddamn selfish," Oscar says out of nowhere.

"What?" Tabor asks.

"Killing himself like that. It fucks up the family."

"He wasn't right," Tabor says.

"I was thinking of my two kids. I can't understand it. It's fucked up."

"No one understands that, do they, Elmer?" Tabor says.

"I suppose not."

"I'm just saying you don't do it in front of your wife and daughter, that's all."

"Camel toe at one o'clock," Tabor says, as a cello-shaped brunette in a yellow blouse and clinking bracelets ambles toward us.

I glance at her over-stretched jeans. He's right.

"It's selfish," Oscar repeats.

"Give the guy a damn break," Tabor says. "He was fucked-up."

Fucked-up. How slowly and unobtrusively it must happen. Does character evaporate like still water? I glance down at the Grand Turk map and know I never want to go there. I like movement. Fast, wide-lane traffic, crowded multiplexes, packed Dolphin games. The older I get the more I like it. About two weeks ago, I pulled across from the middle school one afternoon when class let out, just to see the kids scurry away.

"I can't wait to retire," Oscar says. "I'm countin' the freakin' minutes."

"How much time you got left?" Tabor says.

"Fourteen years."

"You're fucked," Tabor says.

"It goes quick, right?" Oscar says to me.

"That's right." I feel dull thinking about the captain's head resting on the satin pillow, smiling his kayak smile. Why? What's the joke? Maybe it's not a joke, maybe his corners are upturned as an homage to the misbegotten.

"What are you gonna do when you retire?" Tabor says to Oscar.

"Buy a twenty-five foot SeaCraft, a mobile home in Islamorada, and fish, fish, fish."

"I'm moving to Tennessee," Tabor says, "somewhere on a mountain."

"That's my point. You don't off yourself, you find something to do. Christ," Oscar turns to me. "Look at Elmer. The guy's happier than a macaw out of a cage."

I smile.

"You ever see a retired guy *without* a smile on his face?" Oscar says.

"No," I say. Oscar and Tabor talk about Station Two falling apart, one of the guys whose wife caught him with his girlfriend, the iguana placed beneath the rookie's sheets, and how they saved the County's ass at the mutual aid incident a month ago. The words fade as if I'm rafting away from shore. Tabor empties the pitcher in our mugs. I feel the need to do something, to scurry.

A mocha-skinned bartender tilts his head toward the empty pitcher.

"What say you?" Tabor asks us.

Oscar fans his palm, and says, "Not me. I'm on duty tomorrow."

I wouldn't mind another, but I don't say anything.

"What'll we owe?" Tabor says to the bartender.

The guys refuse to take my money. I leave a couple of extra bucks on the bar, tip money, when they're not looking.

Night has replaced day. We shake heartily in the crowded parking lot and Tabor says, "Elmer, great to see you. Sorry it was under these circumstances."

"Likewise."

"Come by the station," he says. "The guys'd love to see you."

"Sure." I'm aware that most of them, who joined after I retired, wouldn't know me. We'd sit around the long, dining table and they'd be courteous because I'm part of the brotherhood, but like all retirees, I'm no longer part of *the* brotherhood. I know, just like Grand Turk, it's not for me.

"Don't do anything stupid," Oscar says, clasping both hands over my one.

"You can't be too stupid and get this old," I say.

"You see?" he says to Tabor. "The old-timers are the best."

We separate, and as I buckle up Oscar taps his horn as he passes in his red F-150. I glance up at the full moon, which looks like a large, pale-white hole drilled through the starless indigo night. Like a hole to heaven. I wonder what I would see if I peeked through?

We're Closing for good Tonight!

It's a forty-minute drive. I should keep going, but the crayoned placard taped to the shabby building yanks at me, and I turn into the nearly vacant lot of the Diamond Lounge. It's a clumsy worn out, suety place no longer relevant to the shimmer of south Florida, much less Hialeah.

I open the glass-framed door, a small bell attached to it rings. The musty a/c-frosted air slaps me. My feet dip into the sticky carpet and my eyes adjust to the dim as I enter the boxcar shaped room. A slim, wrinkled woman in a gray tube top and white shorts is crooked over the pool table located in the back and beneath the pasty glow of an overhanging lamp. She aims her cue stick and arrows it forward. Next to her, a hefty woman with scraggly red hair, wearing a sloppy T-shirt that says *A Guitar and a Gun* dances with herself to "I Think We're Alone Now." I take a seat on a tall leather-bottomed stool near the front and across from the only other patron, a leather-vested, pot-bellied man with long gray hair. He has a pinched face and a bewildered look, as if he's been wondering for the last five decades where the sixties went. He nods and wiggles his mug at me. I notice the grimy, dark-paneled wall behind him is scattered with lighter, frame-shaped outlines. Spaces, I'm guessing, where signs hung, probably taken as mementos.

"Hey there!" a petite, oval-faced woman, about thirty-five,

wearing a ball cap swiveled back so the visor hangs over her wavy-brown pony-tail, says to me in a cracker accent, from behind the bar. "What can I get' cha?"

"J&B with water." She's wearing no make-up, though the pulpy circles beneath her large round eyes look as if they've been brushed with lavender. She's dressed for comfort—jeans and a loose coconut-littered shirt—not for tips. Despite, or maybe because of, her sexual indifference, she is very attractive.

"I believe we can handle that," she says, walking to twin columns of upside-down glasses. She upturns one and pours into it from a nearly empty J&B bottle.

I study the rows of overturned, crystal glasses and the hazy refracted light that skims along their glossy surfaces, shifting color from gold to blue-green. I envision myself kayaking along a foliage-banked, sun-sparkled stream. On one side of the bank stands my father. Not the overweight, double-chinned, fire captain who was buried in his uniform, but the stout, glossy-haired man with the firm, cocky smile. He's dressed in his blue sports jacket, the one he wore when he went out at night. My father smiles his cocky smile and his cologne spices my nostrils. On the other shore I see, even as I'm drifting away, the other captain, my friend, dressed as I last saw him, lying in his coffin. He waves, or is he beckoning? He flashes his kayak smile. Both smiles shake my nerves.

"Last of the JB," the woman says, laying the drink in front of me. "We're closing tonight."

"I saw the sign. How come?"

"Same reason the eight-track died, I suppose."

"Tearing it down?"

"Yap. You'll be able to buy a Whopper here in a few months."

"Bar's been here a long time," I say.

"Over forty years. Feel sorry for the rats." She waves her hand around the room. "They'll be homeless."

I nod, not sure if she's referring to the rodents or the patrons.

She adds, "We all gotta move on," before walking to a double sink near the register. "Holler if you need anything."

She smiles. Her plump cheeks and upturned lips look as

natural, pure and clean as the drink glasses she dips in and out of the steamy water. *Not cocky or anything like a kayak.* I sip my Scotch. The ice rattles . . . the ice rattles. *Why is life subservient to death, death, death, death? Fuck. He was smiling! Why would you do that? No one smiles and does that to themselves, do they? Why would anyone smile? Why would I? Filthy, futile, morose, smile? Death is nothing. Death is everything. Fire engines, sportcoats, rats, honor guards, mistresses, grandkids, brotherhoods, dead, dead, and dead. Dead is nothing. All we have is nothing?* I push my thumb along the sweaty rock glass. *I want to scurry like hell; feel my chest heave, my legs ache, air swamp my lungs because when you stop moving, you die. That makes it easy to rip a butcher knife into your gut, through your intestines and out your spine. I think I understand. But why was he smiling?*

"Because."

I look up quick. The sixties-guy is talking to himself.

"Because," he repeats, scratching his ball of belly.

Is that why you're smiling? Because? Because of nothing? I want badly to be on duty tomorrow, doing morning equipment check, sipping on coffee, hosing down the tarmac. Doing something. I motion to the girl, who smiles her way to me. "What's the damage?" I ask.

"Nothin' sweetie, last night, last J&B."

"A happy funeral."

"New Orleans style."

"How long you been working here?"

"Nearly seven years," she says.

"If you don't mind me asking, what're you gonna do?"

"Well, I guess I'm gonna sleep in tomorrow, maybe go back to school, maybe waitress, maybe kick out my boyfriend, something."

"Something."

"Yes, sir, always gotta keep moving, do something. God helps those who help themselves."

I nod. She takes my glass in her slender fingers and walks to the sink and dips it in the soapy water.

I throw a five on the bar, nod to the sixties guy and leave the dank, windowless, ode to another time.

The humid night bastes my pores. A quick breeze ruffles through my shirt. I glance at the traffic passing from halogen light to halogen light. In the distance a siren wails. *Somewhere, somebody is doing something.* I look up at the pearly drill-hole one final time. *If I tore my way through the hole what would I find? Everything? . . . Nothing? If I was up there looking down, here, what would I see? Something! And something is better than nothing.* I enter my sedan and phone Doris to let her know I'm on my way home.

Lucky

By
Lizabeth Solomon

Mark Matteson, suddenly depressed over how quickly he could burn through his paycheck, knocked on his chest to help himself burp and returned to rolling a joint from the scrap of weed and roaches on the rolling tray in front of him. In the background, the television droned on with a commercial about acid indigestion. Before he rolled up the little stash balanced precariously on an E-Z Wider rolling paper, he picked up the remote with his free hand and flipped the channel—impossible to find anything to watch on a Friday night in the summertime since he'd cancelled his cable. Then again, when he'd had cable, all he got was crap he didn't want to watch anyway. When he ran out for beer, he'd have to hit the video store.

Maureen O'Riley opened her eyes in time to catch the last glint of the sun's rays fading from the evening sky. She hadn't intended to fall asleep, only to rest her throbbing feet a few minutes. Why was it men didn't get picked to wear high heels? It was one of those rhetorical "why me" questions, the kind she knew she must annoy God in asking, and yet it was only one of numerous apparent inequities women seemed fixed to suffer. Maureen slipped off her pantyhose, while she was at it her skirt, and hobbled to the refrigerator while unbuttoning her blouse. She closed her eyes to the slim pickings inside while cool air floated against her body up to her face. A shower would refresh her enough to pick up Chinese and a few movies—after what happened at work, she needed to hibernate.

Mark walked north, a faint smile lifting his face as remembrances of childhood, carefree days when he'd played softball in these streets with his older brother and their pals, breezed through his mind, when everyone called him Lucky. Luke was his given name, but early in life, their baby sister Lucy called him Luck instead, then Lucky. It stuck like crap to the bottom of a shoe.

He wouldn't have minded if he'd ever felt the least bit lucky, but after his brother died young, his parents split up, filling his childhood with disappointments, followed by failed relationships and careers. At some point in his early thirties, it felt like a slap in the face every time he heard his name, so he started telling everyone to call him Mark. It didn't change his luck any, but he felt less obligated to be having a better life than the one he was living. Mark kicked at a stone on the sidewalk and turned up a shadowy gangway leading to his dealer's coach house.

Maureen was annoyed with the black-haired girl at Hunan Palace who sounded far too cheerful to be saying it would be forty minutes before her order was ready. Worse, Maureen watched a young man answering phones slip four orders in front of the cooks before the silly counter-girl got the order straight. Friday night in Chicago— how could she not have called ahead? No sooner did that scratch of self-questioning begin than images from earlier that she'd struggled to wipe from her mind bled through like any scab picked raw.

Teeth clenching, Maureen placed her hand against the stabbing pain in her cheek, tightness creeping down her neck, coiling across her back. Walking or running her magic bullet for ridding her system from angst, she'd donned her athletic shoes even with throbbing feet, but the magic hadn't worked. Stretching her jaw, she birthed a wide yawn. She was going to need that damn dental night guard tonight—her *only* regular bedmate these days.

"Fine." Maureen didn't mean to sound so snappy. "Fine," she repeated, softer, and forced a smile. Puzzlement filled the black eyes of the young girl who ripped the scribbled note from the pad and placed it in line for the cooks. Maureen slipped her handbag strap over her head and hurried off to Jewel and the video store.

Walking up Broadway, she clutched her purse close, eyes darting ahead, watchful for dangers on these boarded-up streets. While, admittedly, everything seemed to annoy her lately, this damn neighborhood annoyed her more than anything. Reminding herself of the investment value, her plan to mushroom the condo into a portfolio of real estate, leveraging its equity once values tripled (*or quadrupled!*), Maureen wished she'd been born into money. She would have made a good heiress.

Two close girlfriends were born into trust funds; Maureen knew all about it. If she were on their financial level, they'd be even closer. As it was, such soul sisters when they did get together, she was occasionally taken along to vacation villas in Puerta Vallarta, on Mediterranean cruises and to parties in Spain. Pussies from the same litter, her old boyfriend had teased one day when they'd all gone drinking together. Her whole life could have been so much happier, *easier*, but it wasn't, and on days like today, it was especially annoying. Maureen held her breath and stepped around a bum passed out in the doorway next to the liquor store. A line out the door; Lotto was up to forty-seven million. She rarely bought a lottery ticket—just look at the people in line for them. But forty-seven *million* seemed worth some effort.

In the morning, she thought. Early. Someplace without a line, give God the chance to fix this egregious mistake and make her the heiress she surely should have been. If not so lucky, a few more years and the corner liquor store would become the corner Starbucks, other young professionals would hang at outdoor tables with magazines and books, her apartment's worth would near half a million. All she had to do was wait, though it was in the waiting that she found herself missing Erik most.

When they first met, back in high school, Maureen thought Erik was the man she'd grow old with—make babies, plot a garden, have barbecues and baptisms, graduations and grandbabies—until that hateful day when he announced he'd quit his assistant manager job at Osco Drugs to take a job hauling garbage.

What she has since referred to as *The Big Fight* ensued.

I *always* wanted a city job—twice the pay, better benefits, he'd said.

He'd done it without telling her. Aside from the risks from bacterial exposure, merely thinking of putrid garbage trucks turned her stomach sour.

Good for raising a family, he said in that blue-collar tone that too often embarrassed her.

Good for raising a family, her voice shrill as she repeated it. He couldn't have thought about their children, playground cruelties—*Dad* the garbage man. What could he talk about when men talked shop? What about the heiresses? How could she make a life with someone who hadn't considered *her* when making such a major decision?

Maureen surrendered that night to arguments driving them apart. *How could she ever want his fingers or tongue inside her again?* It wasn't that she didn't love him, but perhaps it had been a childish love, one without mutual values. Best to let go, walk away, she'd convinced herself. Yet nights like tonight, feeling vulnerable, irritable and alone, the memory of Erik's lovemaking snuck into her empty spots, tickling and taunting in the most annoying ways.

Mark leaned back on the nappy plaid sofa, holding in smoke from the passing spliff and staring at a pile of coke on a mirrored tray in the center of the table, a long powdered line snaking away from it. His dealer always had a regular rotation of Friday night druggies dropping in and out, but when coke got lined out, everyone sat down. Mark hadn't done coke since the eighties. He couldn't really recall at the moment why he'd stopped, probably the money, maybe the advertising—your brain on coke, that fried-egg campaign. After the second snort, something he couldn't quite put his finger on buoyed his spirits, rekindling his love of this soft white powder. And it had gotten so cheap.

Across from him, a woman with a bulging cleavage and handful of twenties and hundreds rolled up a Benjamin. Mark glanced at her pile of cash, the snake tattoo circling her bicep, but he couldn't take his eyes off her breasts. Already protruding from her tight, lace-trimmed purple cami, he was certain a nipple was about to pop. She leaned across the table, held one nostril closed, the rolled bill in her other hand, and in one fluid movement tossed her long brown hair over her shoulder and inhaled half the line.

Glancing up with a grin that said she knew he'd been watching, she winked and sat back. Heat flashed through his body turning his face beet red.

"Gotcha." She pointed and laughed. Her friends laughed too.

His dealer laughed, until the chesty chick stood up, bills in hand, and signaled him into the next room.

Her friend sat down and handed Mark the joint. "White rhino."

"Rhino, Haze, who cares what it's called as long as it kicks me somewheres into next week." Mark toked, listening as the girl shared a druggy tale about Pink Floyd and a weekend on mushrooms.

When she finished speaking, she rested her hand on Mark's thigh, palm up as if asking for the joint, but he was instantly aroused. Mousy brown hair, a splotchy complexion—that mattered if they were going out, not where his thoughts were heading. Before he could find a way past superficial chitchat, her friend returned holding a brown bag instead of cash.

"Let's go, Betty Jo," she commanded, and they were gone.

Mark shook it off, taking a couple grams of coke with his ounce of smoke. Why the fuck not? he said, as if he had a thousand hundreds like the last ones being peeled from the cash in his pocket. Mark walked to the video store feeling an exuberance he hadn't felt in years, for no apparent reason but the recreational drugs coursing through his veins.

The later it got, the less crap was left on the shelves, and though most of it was crap when it got right down to it, he'd rather get the better crap—new releases first, then the back room. Craving the soft skin of a real woman, hard porn would have to be his weekend bitch instead. Besides, the latest-porn-seen was always good for chatting up the guys on whatever job he got assigned.

Mark used to work regular jobs, but he hated the forced relationships. First it'd be drinks, then dinner, birthdays, holidays. Next, someone would expect him to invite them over—that shit. After Cindy left, Mark wanted to live however-the-fuck Mark wanted to live. He didn't want anyone coming over; he didn't want to have to explain himself. Working day-labor jobs got rid of that social bullshit. He lived for weekends with cases of beer and ounces of pot, sobering up for work, but as time passed, extending past weekends into a way of life.

Blow-em-up flicks were perfect to get lost in, Mark thought, scanning for action movies, that Steven Seagal flick he'd heard was out. Then he noticed her: long white legs sticking out from running shorts that would have been longer on shorter women, thick red hair pulled back and hanging halfway down her back. God, he hated women like her, like Irish girls he'd grown up with who'd stomped on his florescent longings as if they'd been weeds. He grabbed *Out of Reach* from New Releases, *Under Siege 2: Dark Territory* from Manager's Picks on the next shelf and ducked into the back room.

Fighting the tension in her jaw, Maureen knew a laugh-out-loud comedy was her DOC tonight, her drug of choice, the fix she needed to anesthetize the pain of her life. Romantic comedy, something to help picture a happy ending. Maureen chose two sets of rent-two-get-the-third-free picks in no time. As fast as she was, there was an annoyingly long line to check out. Forced to stand still, even in her best Nikes, her pups were *sore*. Perusing previously-viewed movies and over-priced candies, she recalled how she'd scold Erik for wasting money on such junk.

It wasn't the money as much that he let himself be manipulated—giant conglomerates controlling him through marketing spin and merchandising strategies, she'd rant, threatening to annoy him. Until finally, he'd look at her—one look, and it tended to silence her. Not because he'd be angry. Rather, he looked bored, or maybe it was pity that she troubled over things so trivial. With a glance instead of words, he said, So? If he wanted Mike and Ike's or the pop and popcorn deal, why care if he made some marketing geek's week? Maureen wished for a do-over on the girl she'd been back then.

Her attention pulled back to the moment by the sensation of someone staring, she turned to catch the eye of an Adonis. He looked away immediately, making it Maureen's turn to stare— bulging biceps, broad shouldered, blond hair, a face in perfect balance with full, very kissable lips.

When Mark turned around, Maureen was smiling. Eyes piercing past her facade, he returned her smile with a nod.

All her nooks and crevices suddenly moist, way out of her comfort zone, she faced front.

Why did she go and smile then turn away? He knew her type: she'd either want to change him or reject him. Besides, what would he say to a chick like that? If you aren't doing anything later, want to wrap those legs around my neck? God, he'd like to taste the meaty white flanks of this lovely lass, but shit, he'd have a better chance winning the lotto.

At Jewel, Mark browsed, searching for something to satisfy him that he knew wasn't stocked in these aisles, but he didn't really have anywhere else to go. And then he spotted her again, picking out ice cream. Some women could draw him like a screw to a magnetic drill tip. He'd never think of the right thing to say to a girl like her—because all he wanted was to fuck her senseless. And how do you say *that* to a woman like *that*?

Chicks he picked up at bars got shit-faced right along with him. Knowing they were juiced, he'd sidle in close at the jukebox and just-like-that say, "You wanna fuck?" You'd think he'd have proposed marriage, they'd be so happy. He picked fun ones— tramps, good for a night. None he'd play house with for real. Not that he *wanted* to get serious, but he could almost change his ways for a girl like Red over there. If only he could think of the right shit to say, small talk *bull*shit, but what? Fucking formalities. Porn was so much easier. Besides, what did he have to offer anybody but a brood of bad habits and a growing stack of debts?

Watching her wristwatch, Maureen stayed focused. Aside from ice cream, nothing unhealthy. At Sunday mass, she heard God promise that the man of her dreams would be along before long. She wanted to be ready. Maureen gazed longingly at pizza, cookies, potato chips, Pepsi, and passed them by.

Another line. Two carts in front of hers and the cashier switched her light to flash. Exasperated, Maureen picked up *People* and began flipping pages. The manager is at another register picking up cash. Whatever the problem, Maureen wants to fix it. She once believed she could fix all sorts of things, but for now it was all she could do to stay afloat at the firm she'd joined. The opportunity curiously presented itself at the same time she split with Erik. She'd taken it as a sign to leave her public defender post, her heart wasn't in it anyway, and make a strategic design for upward mobility.

Private practice proved more of a challenge than she'd ever imagined. Struggling to find her niche, Maureen's billable hours fell to the lowest in the firm, and she was given a gift, an account from one of the partners. With every element of a life raft to it, she grabbed hold gratefully. Billable hours would be something colleagues worried about.

The client was likeable, a Woody Allen look-a-like with a pleasant smelling pipe. Armed with research about his companies and rise to success, Maureen attempted to impress him. They lunched at the Executive Club, spending hours discussing how he'd become the mogul he now was. Back at her office, he aggressed that *he* knew his legal needs better than she. He would dictate; she would administrate.

He leaned close. Maureen expecting a workplace kiss, perhaps an apology, offered her cheek. Instead he jabbed his tongue between her lips and grabbed at her, moving her hand to his privates. His companies needed all sorts of things *drawn up*, he whispered before she pulled her hand away. He sneered, a sneer that said her law degree was laughable, that said they were all prostitutes—only currencies changed.

Rising to her feet, she'd hoped to intimidate him with her height, but he buried his face to her chest. She pushed him away. Incorrigible, she scolded, as she strode to her office door and opened it for him to go.

Obsessing over each detail, she wondered whether the gift had been extended with strings she'd failed to see. Maureen returned the magazine in her hand to the rack and absentmindedly rubbed her hand over her forehead while she glanced across the store, the other lines all longer. A wine display caught her eye—exactly what she needed.

Mark knew better than to go to the grocery store when he was high and hungry, but here he was—Cheetos, Lay's Potato Chips, Totino's pizzas, movie-theatre-style-buttered popcorn, Oreos, Eli's cheese cake, a two-pack of steaks, sandwich meats, cheeses, Italian bread, a case of Miller, mixed nuts, milk, chocolate milk, Coke, Heavenly Hash ice cream, and a bag of salad. He rolled his cart toward the checkout and felt his blood drop to his feet. Cupid on the job, the red-haired woman from the video store was standing before him. Sliding his cart behind hers, more than his blood rose.

Glancing into her cart he spotted nasty alfalfa sprouts, s*kim* milk, that soy shit. No guy in his right mind'd drink that crap. *So that meant she was single.* A half-gallon of fancy fresh orange juice from the produce department, Godiva ice cream. All about money, like every other chick he'd known any length of time. Work hard to make *them* happy—fuck that. He barely wanted to work to make himself happy.

But, her fragrance—floral, like the scent on Cindy's pillow long after she'd left. Mark loved and missed all at once that sweetly scented sweat only women possess. He closed his eyes, unaware of leaning closer as he breathed her scent in deeper, not caring whatever bullshit he'd have to jump through just to touch her.

Maureen noticed the smell first. Cigarette smoke, but that distinct tinge of reefer and dirty bong water. She'd stopped smoking pot when Erik left. Well, when she ran out of the pot he'd left behind. Being an attorney, she didn't want anyone to know she smoked pot, but admittedly, she missed it sometimes, like she sometimes missed Erik.

Maureen turned to see the handsome guy from the video store and her heart skipped. This close he bore a resemblance to Brad Pitt, a kind of Brad Pitt/Kevin Costner combination. A little weathered, more like in *Snatch* or *Tin Cup* than on the red carpet, but so appealing that it was hard *not* to stare, impossible not to smile.

Is she laughing at me, or flirting? Mark nodded, raised an eyebrow and considered the rap he'd use on a greased night in a bar. She'd get real fast if he said something like that, but even so and even if, what was the point? Eventually the only conversation they'd have is what she wanted to decorate, paint, clean, or buy. Why torture himself? Easy—if only to hold her.

"These lines. You'd think they could afford more help." Maureen noticed all the junk food in his cart, all that beer, this was no guy for her. Porn flicks inside the video bag, no doubt. No. No. … but those arms. God how she'd like to lose herself in those biceps for a night, plus the rest of his muscle mass.

She followed his eyes to her legs. Shifting her weight, she glanced over to find herself distracted by how well he filled out his jeans. Maureen felt that smile come across her face, the same enticing smile that edged her ahead of friends when flirting, and though she told herself she was being friendly, she couldn't rope in her smile. Extending her tongue to unsmile her lips, folding them inward, using her teeth to bite them down, they kept smiling.

Was this a come on, Mark wondered just as Maureen reasoned, *What if he were Jesus?*

Sunday school lessons from long ago woven into Maureen's logic provided safe haven in more ways than first spun, yet she knew Jesus would not be wearing a cloak of cigarette and pot smoke. The cashier processing the order ahead, Maureen began to unload her cart.

"What?" Mark asked, so caught up in watching Maureen lick her lips that he'd barely registered she'd spoken. She had beautiful, translucent skin, the kind you could see blue veins behind, and such white teeth, those dancing green eyes. Like he was looking into his own eyes but true and good. A girl like her, speaking to him—was he so stoned he was hallucinating?

"What did you say?"

Maureen nodded. "The lines—"

"Brutal."

"You were at the video store, right?"

"Oh, right. Yeah." Mark leaned back, trying to act cool but felt lame, out of practice as he attempted to read her face. Not a word back. "So, … uh … you live in the neighborhood?"

Maureen was aroused by how deeply his voice resonated. "Sunnyside, The Lofts."

"I gutted that place."

Her eyes opened like a window.

"Demolition crew. Was my old grammar school, boarded up for years."

Maureen, feeling drawn, teased. "Demolition get-back for all those detentions?"

"Haha." Flattered by her interest, he kept talking. "So where in the building? The gym? Nurse Wilson's office overlooking those golden linden trees? I spent plenty of time visiting her." Mark felt dumb as soon as he said it, but Maureen chuckled.

She loved watching those lindens outside her kitchen window, sparkling like gold coins when the sun caught them just so.

Encouraged by her laughter, he laughed himself, revealing teeth in dire need of whitening and a cracked side tooth

Why couldn't he have better teeth? And what was she doing telling a stranger where she lived? Despite something vaguely endearing, there was no future here. Was she only attracted to losers? Was something wrong with her? Before she could give these frightening questions serious contemplation, the line was moving.

"It's a solid building. I can tell you that." Mark's arm brushed hers as he lifted his beer onto the conveyor next to her ice cream.

The hair on his forearm was surprisingly soft, sensual, rendering Maureen momentarily dizzy. She grabbed at the conveyor belt to steady herself, placing her hands on the cold ice cream and moving it to the front of her order. "Hope this isn't melted before I get home."

Mark heard but didn't believe she gave one shit about the ice cream. He wanted to offer her a beer, a few, invite her over, get to know each other better, but what would she say? *Call me.* God, he hated that bullshit.

He wanted to say, "Leave your ice cream and come home with me—share mine. Do you like Heavenly Hash?" He pictured them flesh-to-flesh with only ice cream and a spoon between them and chuckled at the thought. Maureen looked confused. He pointed to his own ice cream.

"I was thinking the same thing." Good, Mark, good, he told himself. Chicks dig that *I-was-thinking-the-same-thing* shit.

Maureen's smile returned. She rolled her lips together, trying to relax her cheeks as she reached for the bar to place behind her order.

"You're going to die early if you keep eating that way." Noticing his artery-clogging consumables, she'd been unable to resist, and they both heard the call-to-play of her tone.

"I'll die happy," Mark quipped. "'Course, there are a couple other ways I'd rather die, given a choice."

Maureen felt the heat of his body so near that her cheeks turned crimson and her brain short-circuited. She knew what he meant, and she was in just the frame of mind that ... but the ringing of the register as the cashier moved her groceries through was like an alarm waking her. Maureen watched each price flash as if making sure the register didn't err, but she was struggling for to what to say. Entering the total on her check, she handed it over with her Jewel card, and said nothing. While waiting for the electronic system to finish processing, she turned to gaze at the handsome stranger one last time.

"Well, have a good night." Maureen lifted her two bags and left. At Hunan Palace, her Pad Thai chicken and spring rolls were waiting. Securing the warm package away from her ice cream, she hurried home.

As Mark watched her leave, his heart dropped. Something in her eyes made him feel special. Maybe they'd bump into each other again. Was that why she told him where she lived? Hell, he'd stroll that way *tonight*. Mark took his change, groceries and trudged out the automatic doors, thoughts of Maureen sporadically flashing through his body like weak fluorescent lights.

At the corner liquor store, Mark stopped for rolling papers and a lottery ticket. It was a rollover, somewheres in the neighborhood of forty, fifty mill, he'd heard. He gave the clerk a ten and got eight bucks of quick-picks—what the fuck? Maybe he'd get lucky. If he did hit it, he'd buy himself a condo in that same crib as the red-haired girl. He'd dress up nice—one of those fine leather jackets, good cologne, really *wow* that babe. She wouldn't be in such a hurry to scurry *then*. With that, he tried to put her out of his mind.

But Maureen didn't leave so easily. Mark normally waited to put on porn flicks until much later, but that bitch inflamed his loins. He opened a beer, threw a few in the freezer, unwrapped a pizza and tossed it in the oven. He took a hit off his bong, popped in flick one and lay back with his free hand unzipping his pants while watching impromptu orgies spring from innocent camping scenes on his forty-two inch TV. Ten minutes later, the pizza was done and so was his first orgasm.

Back home, Maureen no longer wanted to watch movies. That man had unsettled her, calling out animal urges she generally kept leashed. Unpacking the wine, she suddenly wished she'd had a glass or two *before* she'd run into him. Stirred up beyond being able to sit still, she took a couple bites from a spring roll, left the rest of the food on the table, grabbed her car keys, a bottle of water, and headed to the gym.

An hour on the Stairmaster and this would be out of her system, she told herself, ignoring her aching feet while eyeing her figure in the mirrors on the opposite wall with approval. The right man would be along before long, she reminded herself, peeking around at the men working out, just not tonight.

By the end of the first Steven Seagal movie, one pizza, a couple-few beers, joints, lines later, Mark felt himself a hero. Grabbing his Vaseline Intensive Care, he told himself that *when* he got to know Red, he'd definitely take her camping. He rewound the porn flick, sensations and images sifting through him, Maureen's face haunting him, picturing her white legs around him, his face buried in them. He staggered into the kitchen for the Heavenly Hash ice cream and his *other* stash of heavenly hash. He opened a tin box on the table, unwrapped a piece of foil, sliced the small tar-like ball, placed it in the bowl of his pipe and fired, pulling the smoke deep into his lungs.

Mark held the smoke tight in his chest, traveling in his mind to the street where Maureen lived, imagining her smile, licking those lips. What was *that* all about if she wasn't hot for him? Women. Maybe you had to grab them, like in the days of cavemen, club them over the head and make them your own. Not that he'd actually do that, but God forgive him for some of his thoughts. He let out a long, slow exhale that left him lightheaded. He'd have to see her again. But first, he had to pee.

Mark staggered to the bathroom and sat down to pee, too buzzed to stand with any hope of streaming straight. He sat longer than needed, distractedly fondling himself while thinking of Maureen. Finally he rose, stood at the sink, splashed water on his face, combed his hair and determined he was too fucked up, not to walk over there, the fresh air'd help that, but he *looked* fucked up, his eyes. He wanted to impress her not scare her. He'd wait, maybe a morning walk. Sure. Refreshed, rested, a fresh start to more than just the day.

Mark walked over to Maureen's building the next day and the next, but only in his mind. All weekend long, he administered doses of his favorites drugs and masturbated to fantasies of Maureen's silky red tresses falling all about him, of her riding close on top of him in the cramped confines of their tent, smothering him with her body. His excitement heightened, visions of her soft white skin sliding against his leg instead of his own arm, the bare skin of her breast flush against his face instead of his own pillow.

Maureen normally looked forward to work, but today, clouded from movies and too much wine, she dreaded facing the fallout from Friday. Riding the Ravenswood train downtown, she tried blocking the torrid memories pushing through her hangover by sorting stacks of papers she'd dragged home but never touched. Her wandering mind caused her to give up, and that was when she heard everyone talking about one single *locally*-sold ticket winning all six numbers, all fifty-five million. Maureen prayed it was hers.

But her ticket had not even a single matching number, and the client-gift vanished in an e-mail from the partner explaining that the client had chosen an associate with more experience in commercial leasing. When Friday arrived, Maureen was more ready than ever to escape into fictional realities again. She'd forced herself not to think about those eyes that looked as if they'd been undressing her, but now, she searched around, hoping to see the handsome stranger, while she grabbed *Troy*, *Meet Joe Black* and *Bull Durham* off the shelves. A shorter line than she wanted and more chatter about the lottery: the winning ticket, the cashier boasted to the woman ahead of her, was sold at the liquor store around the corner.

Of all the stupid lines, Maureen scolded herself, why not there?

That night she fell asleep watching Brad Pitt's naked butt and woke remembering erotic dreams with the stranger. She drove to the gym, worked out for two hours, cooled down with a Grasshopper and zoned out in the steam room. On the way home, she stopped at Manny's Pancake House for breakfast. She grabbed a stool at the counter, the TV above airing breaking news—the winner of last week's lottery had turned up dead. A dispute was ensuing over the winnings.

Instinctively, Maureen knew this case was hers. She left twenty dollars on the counter, dropped a ten in a panhandler's cup outside and went home to plan. Searching her newspapers for an article, obit, anything leading to more information, there it was: Luke "Lucky" Matteson, 38, also known as Mark, dead nearly a week before his only sister found him. A massive coronary possibly caused by asphyxiation. *Asphyxiation?* Maureen puzzled. No foul play was indicated. The ticket was in the sister's possession, but the landlord was claiming halves, as was a woman identifying herself as a girlfriend. Maureen traced the sister to an address near Belmont and Pulaski and drove straight there, sensing the best tactic was to show up and start talking.

A large-boned, overweight woman with eyes swollen from crying answered the door. Maureen identified herself as an attorney and began to tell Lucy she could protect her from the bogus claims mentioned in the paper and other unscrupulous deals that would be coming at her. Lucy hesitated, but there was something in Maureen's eyes that reminded her of Lucky. They were green like his, but there was something else, something she couldn't quite put her finger on.

Lucy opened the screen door and invited Maureen inside. She made coffee, and the two of them sat in an old-fashioned kitchen overlooking a backyard strung with clotheslines, chatting like old friends until Maureen had Lucy's life story and a new client.

Grabbing a childhood photo off the living room table as they walked to the front door, Lucy said, "He would have liked you." Her heart felt as if her brother had brought this angel to her. "It's as if you were heaven sent."

Maureen embraced Lucy, holding her close for a moment or so. How hard it must be to lose both brothers, she pondered, and lingered at the door. Maureen took the framed photo in hand and studied little Luke and Lucy, not quite teenagers, and suddenly, she knew.

"Do you have another? More recent?"

Lucy grabbed a pack of photos off a nearby shelf.

Maureen knew before she saw the photo—it was the stranger from the video store. Tears filled her.

"I'm so sorry," Maureen said finally.

Too bad they hadn't met, Lucy thought, touched by Maureen's emotion. Maybe her brother wouldn't have been so lonesome. Fighting away the image of how she'd found him, she focused on the innocuous photograph instead. Maybe, she's thought many times since, maybe he wouldn't be so dead.

Outside, Maureen rested her head to her steering wheel and sobbed. She couldn't say why, but she felt like a bad Christian, like she'd turned her back on Christ, and unworthy of His love, here He was saving her professional ass.

"What was I supposed to do?" She tilted her head upward.

Maureen heard no reply but felt calmed by the silence.

Wiping tears from her face, she recalled the provocative comment Lucy's brother had made. She replayed it in her mind like a scene from a favorite movie. In the replay, she added lines she'd thought to say on her way home that night, lines that had followed his lead and found them back at her place instead.

Maureen sensed, believed, he'd thought of her too. She paused, trying to grasp the mystery of it all. If God was counting on her to save this man, surely she had failed. Head hung, Mark's face returned to her mind's eye, and she couldn't help but smile. She would have called him Lucky, she thought, her mind filling with things she might have said, intimacies they might have shared.

"Now there's a dreamboat," she noted to the empty car and pulled away from the curb.

Swimming Against the Weimaraner

By
David Beaty

The girls came out of the water. We boys had moved up while the girls were racing, and now, under a summer sun that beat like hot velvet on our eleven-and-twelve-year-old heads, we waited behind the starting blocks on rickety metal chairs. In front of us lay the pool, mysterious, blue and frightful.

Kim won her heat. She pulled herself onto the pool deck and staggered towards me. I raised her lucky Winnie-the-Pooh towel to my nose and sniffed sunlight, chlorine, coconut oil, sweat. She took her towel. Water dripped off her cropped red hair and down her freckled arms and legs. Her red Speedo clung to her. Her hand trailed across my shoulder.

The starter, Hose Nose Rosen, called out, "Boys up next."

I waited by my starting block. It was a Saturday afternoon at the tired end of August. I was a few days shy of my thirteenth birthday, and this was the last big swimming event of the summer, the Florida Junior Olympics, held that year at the old Casino pool in Ft. Lauderdale, across A1A from the beach. My next race was a semifinal heat of the two hundred yard individual medley for my age group. We had to swim two laps each of butterfly, backstroke, breaststroke and freestyle, in that order.

Coach, passing, winked and gave me a thumbs-up.

"Coach, please, I've got to talk to you."

He paused, scrutinizing me. "Can it wait until you win this heat?"

I nodded. He went and stood where he could see the finish.

I was assigned lane two. Richie Alfers was in lane four. Between us was Billy Cardozo, who didn't count. Richie Alfers was my problem. He'd beaten me every time we raced.

I called Richie "the Weimaraner." He had the Weimaraner's ash-colored hair, and those eerie, light-colored eyes, and the Weimaraner's nervous, hang-dog expression.

My parents were too busy to come to my swimming meets. They liked it when I won, but my failures in the pool were my own business. Richie's parents came to every meet. His father, a fat man in a Dodgers baseball cap, cornered Richie before and after every race, jabbing a finger at his chest. Richie's mother, short and sharp-featured, argued over Richie's official results; whenever our paths crossed, she flashed me a "Why don't you drop dead?" look. When Richie raced, she leaned out of the bleachers near the finish, stopwatch in hand, shrilling like a TV Comanche.

A judge blew his whistle, and we climbed onto our starting blocks. I saw the starting pistol hanging from Rosen's right hand. He was a genial, skinny man. He covered his famous nose with white zinc cream. Everybody knew he was a fast starter.

Billy Cardozo and I wished each other good luck. Then Billy and I wished Richie Alfers good luck. As usual, he ignored us. It was bad luck to be unsporting, but I worried Richie was stronger than luck.

I stepped to the front of my starting block. Water sparkled below me. Over me sailed the faint white ghost of the moon. Voices died away. Now I had to beat Richie Alfers, or at least swim fast enough to get a lane next to him in the finals tonight. I needed to *see* him when we raced tonight, so I could go faster.

"Swimmers," Rosen called. "On your marks."

I went into my starting crouch. I imagined myself unwinding, hands reaching for the other end of the pool and a better life. The pistol fired just as I came out of the low point of my crouch. Rosen had started us fast again, and I'd timed it just right.

I landed in an explosion of sunlight and bubbles. My arms rose into the "U" of the butterfly stroke, my head lifted, but I wouldn't breathe.

The cheering started in my head. During a race, or practice, even when I was swimming alone, I imagined the bleachers filled with people cheering for *me*. Bobby! Go, Bobby Talbot!

I swam four stroke cycles before I breathed. Looking up, I saw a smear of sky, bleachers, waving arms. When I came out of the turn, all I could think about how tired my arms felt, and how choppy the water was.

At the other end of the pool I'd switch to backstroke and give my muscles a change. *Just a few yards till the backstroke. Just a few yards, just a few yards.*

As I came off the wall into the backstroke, I saw Richie. I was ahead. But he was moving up, his backstroke powerful, and without thinking my attitude began to change. Through the backstroke, the breaststroke, the freestyle, I swam the way I'd swum against the Weimaraner all summer: At some point in every race, I gave up swimming to win, and swam *not to lose.*

At the finish, I touched the wall, gasping, looking over for Richie. Coach's crew-cut head loomed next to my starting block. He held up two fingers. *Second place.* He raised his stopwatch in one hand and a thumb in the other, and smiled.

Second place. Second best. And somebody yelled that Richie had broken a national record. Up on the pool deck, his mother and father were hugging him, whooping and jumping. A disgusting sight. My parents would never rush onto the pool deck to congratulate me.

Richie's parents were making all the noise, not Richie. The more I watched the Weimaraner family, the stranger their celebration seemed. Richie stared gloomily over his mother's shoulder, while his father's slab-like hand pounded congratulations on his head. Where was the winner's joyous look, like the one I'd seen on Kim? Richie looked as if breaking a national record only made his life worse.

I smiled at Richie. He seemed to read my mind, because he saw my mean little smile, and a look of understanding passed between us, though I didn't quite understand it. I looked away.

Coach congratulated me. He was a powerful man, my height, all chest and long arms. "Great! You're just where you want to be."

"Second place?"

"You're only three-tenths of a second behind. You broke the national record, too. You've got him worried."

"Sure."

"Take my word for it. He's worrying."

I thought about the frozen, unhappy look on Richie's face.

I almost questioned Coach about it, but decided to keep my discovery--that's how I saw it--to myself.

Coach told me to relax until evening. Eat early, he said. Call your mother.

That's when I lied. I wasn't a liar, most of the time, but now I told Coach I'd talked to my mom, and she'd said it was okay if I lived with Barbara and him when school started. Lying made me feel a little breathless. I said, "So--is that okay?"

He held up a hand, as if stopping traffic. He asked, Is that what you wanted to talk to me about before the race? I nodded. He frowned, looked away. He said, I'm beginning to wonder about you. Did you really call your mother? He didn't believe me. He asked if I needed money to call. I said I'd called. Listen, he said. You call her right now. I'll check up on you. Tell her you're swimming like a champ. Tell her to come up tonight to see you win the gold. Are you listening?

I asked him again if I could live with Barbara and him when school started. Coach sighed. He said, My friend, we've got to get you right with your mama. Okay? That's first. He patted me on the shoulder. Stay out of the sun, he said. Keep those muscles loose. Anything you need, I'm around. The kids are up in the bleachers. Hang out there. Around five, take a light warm-up, fifty laps or so. Finals start at seven. Come to me before, we'll go over your race. Now go call your mama. I nodded.

He regarded me for a long moment before he moved on. I didn't want him to go. The pool deck was emptying; spectators had already left the stands. I felt lonely, dissatisfied with myself. I looked around for Kim.

The minutes before a race were always wonderful. That was the best time. After a race, I grieved. I felt hollow. No matter how well I'd swum, I always thought I hadn't swum fast enough. And, at the same time, I feared I'd never swim as fast again. I had no idea where my talent came from--it disappeared at the end of every race. That was my guilty secret. After a race, I felt worthless, a fraud. At the same time, I wanted to rebuild my life through swimming, because it was the only talent I had. I could only hope for the world's love and support by swimming well, even though I knew that would probably--no, certainly--never happen again.

Mr. Alfers loomed up, chewing gum. His Keds lacked laces, his madras shorts sagged. He wore his Dodgers baseball cap pulled low over his eyes. He dropped a hand on my shoulder. "Where's your mama? Where's your poppa?"

"At home." He knew they never came to a swim meet.

"And you such a good boy. Not a bad swimmer, neither. But not--" he squeezed my shoulder so hard, it hurt-- "not as good as my Richie."

I shook my shoulder free of his hand. "Why don't you leave him alone?"

He'd been about to grab me again, but now he dropped his hand and blinked at me.

My remark surprised me, too.

"Hey, I'm *Richie's* papa." He sounded sorry for himself. "I love my boy."

"We see you." I don't know what I meant, but I felt a little crazy saying it.

Mr. Alfers' eyes bugged out. He asked who in the goddamned hell I thought *I* was.   He reached out again.

I dodged his hand. My legs felt shaky, but they got me away. I climbed into the stands, where my team had pitched camp.

McInerney called out to me, "Way to go in the medley, Bobby!" He raised a long arm in salute. He'd broken a national record in the backstroke that morning.

My teammates were lying between the bleachers, reading, eating sandwiches, or sleeping. I felt hungry. Coach had advised me to eat sooner, not later. I reclaimed my airline bag from Brundage, who'd placed second in the breaststroke trials, and studied the pool deck for Mr. Alfers. I didn't see him, but I waited to make sure. I wondered where Kim was. She swam with the Allapattah Y team. I was always looking for Kim that summer. Now the summer was almost over, I was afraid she'd disappear forever.

I took a T-shirt, jeans and sneakers from my airline bag, dressed, and walked around the corner to a Rexall drugstore for lunch. I looked for Kim, but the lunchroom was empty. The air was thick with cigarette smoke, which the overhead fans slowly pushed around. I sat at the long red Formica counter with my paperback copy of *A Tale of Two Cities,* a book that was on my summer reading list. I ordered a cheeseburger, fries, and a large glass of milk. I wondered what Richie Alfers ate for lunch. Probably some weird and potent drink his mother whipped up for him that gave off a cold smoke, like dry ice, when she poured it into a polished silver mug for him.

After lunch, I went to a telephone booth at the far end of the Formica counter and called home. The phone rang. Finally, my mother picked up. I heard Doris Day singing in the background. I said, "It's Bobby."

"Bobby who?"

This was an old routine of hers and I hated it.

"Bobby, your son."

"Just a minute." She yelled, "For God's sake, Phillip, turn that *down*."

My mother used to say I hung around home too much. "Don't you have any friends?" Saturday afternoons she called "*My special time.*" She slept late on Saturday mornings and Phillip, my second stepfather, a pilot for Pan American, played tennis. In the evenings, they drank martinis and danced to Doris Day and Rosemary Clooney records (his choice), or Frank Sinatra (hers). Afterwards, they fought.

That year they fought about Jean. When Phillip was flying, Jean came to our house in Mariola Court to tend the garden. My mother said Jean was a *much* better handyman than Phillip. Afterwards, she stayed for martinis and supper. Sometimes she stayed over.

When Phillip and my mother fought about Jean, my mother would storm up the stairs and slam their bedroom door, leaving Phillip to sit staring out the French doors at the back yard. Now and then she'd break something while he smoked and finished the pitcher of martinis and hummed along with Doris Day or Rosemary Clooney. Then, sighing, he'd climb the stairs to my mother.

I was afraid Phillip would leave for good, like my father, and like Anthony, my first stepfather. My mother got very sad after they left. I remembered the silent, darkened house, worrying about food, avoiding the telephone. Her car parked askew in the driveway. Lying to the neighbors. Missing school.

When I went to live with Coach and his wife Barbara, I swam on Saturdays.

My mother said, "Where are you this time?"

"Fort Lauderdale. It's the Florida Junior Olympics. I broke a national record and I placed second in the semifinals for the two hundred yard individual medley. I was only three-tenths of a second off first place."

"Congratulations, darling."

"Three-tenths of a second is nothing."

"Of course not, darling, but wasn't the whole idea of you living with Coach this summer and training all day that you'd come in . . . first?"

I was sweating. I slid open the phone booth's folding door to let in some air. "It's only three-tenths of a second between us."

I could feel her interest going away. "What's that *noise*?"

"I just shut the phone booth door." I leaned my forehead against the glass. It felt cool. "The finals are tonight. Are you going to come up?"

"I'll certainly try."

I missed her terribly and got this urge to say I'd give up living with Coach and Barbara, that I'd quit practicing six hours a day, that I'd come home tomorrow.

But then I thought about going home when school started. I didn't want to leave the life I'd had that summer.

I belonged to a team. We worked out three hours every morning, ate lunch and took a nap, then worked out another three hours, ate dinner, and fell into bed. That was the life I wanted. I couldn't avoid going back to school, but I *hated* the thought of spending another Saturday afternoon listening to my mother and Phillip fight.

"Coach wants me to live with Barbara and him."

"You are already."

"During the school year."

My mother's voice carried a warning tone. "You're only twelve, dear. You need a normal life, not just swimming, swimming, swimming. You've done wonderfully well this summer. But enough is enough."

"Coach says I have a shot at the Olympic team in four years."

"Aren't we getting ahead of ourselves?"

"I'm just telling you what Coach said."

"No one's doubting you. Or him. He's very inspiring. That's his job. We could just as well say that you have *a shot* at being the first American in outer space. That's also true. First, though, we have more mundane matters to get through. Like eighth grade."

"Are you going to come up tonight? Finals begin at seven."

"I'll let Phillip know. A big, big kiss for you, darling."

I sat for a while, thinking, *I failed*. When I came out, I saw that the glass panels on the telephone booth had fogged up. I shivered.

I went back to the bleachers and slept until the late afternoon. After I woke, I went downstairs and used the bathroom. Out in the entrance hallway, I saw Richie Alfers walking towards the exit and, without thinking, called out, "Hey, Richie!"

He halted and looked around at me.

"Way to go this morning in the individual medley." I meant it, too, at least in the moment I was saying it. But then I wondered, Why praise my enemy? I had spoken without thinking. Now I felt embarrassed.

He stared at me as if he was expecting me to say something mean or snarky. Not hearing anything like that, he frowned, turned, and walked out to the street.

"I'm going for a walk on the beach," Kim said, coming out of the women's bathroom, her lucky Winnie-the-Pooh towel draped over her shoulders.

"Can I come, too?"

We crossed A1A and walked down to the beach, to where the sand was wet and easier to walk on. Kim asked how long I'd been swimming in competition. Two years, I said. I asked about her. "Same thing. My grandmother sent me down to the Allapattah Y pool." Kim smiled. "She thought it would keep me out of trouble." I said I never wanted to stop swimming in competition. Why? Kim said. I said, "Because I feel good when I'm racing and bad when I stop. I was always really dopey in football and baseball. Then Coach arrived. He told me that if I swam hard I'd be a champion. Everybody else was telling me I'd always be a jerk. Now the only person who treats me like that is Richie Alfers."

"Well, you're better than Richie Alfers."

She took my hand. I almost tripped over a piece of driftwood. We were holding hands! We kept on walking.

I said, So why do you swim? To get out of my house, she said. I hate it, she said. I don't want it. How, I wondered, could a kid "want" or "not want" their house? Is it haunted? I said. Kind of, she said. It's mine, but I can't sell it until I go to college. Doesn't your mother want it? She died. What about your father? He died, too. They died together? She died in the hospital in Miami. He was an Air Force pilot. I was born in Germany, she said. He flew Shooting Stars, F-80s. I *know* what an F-80 is, I said. I've got a bunch of books about fighter jets at home. Kim said, He got shot down in Korea by a Russian. I was three. My mother remarried and we moved back here. After she died, and my stepfather left, my grandparents moved in.

I told Kim that my father was an Air Force pilot, too, but now he sold insurance in Chicago. My stepfather was a pilot for Pan Am. He flew to Rio and Buenos Aires.

We were silent for a while, and then Kim said, "Okay, truth time. Why do you let Richie psych you out?"

"What do you mean?"

"I see how he puts you down. I see how it gets to you."

"He's the champion. He comes in first. I come in second."

"He's a sick asshole. I feel sorry for him."

"What do you know about Richie Alfers?"

"I know what you know."

"Who says I know anything?"

"I'm not blind. You've figured him out. Why do you let him psych *you* out?"

I blurted, "I'm pretty sure his papa beats him if he doesn't swim fast enough."

There--it was out, the "discovery" I'd been carrying around all day. Saying it gave me a thrill of excitement, but it left me feeling slightly nauseated.

Kim stepped in front of me, forcing me to halt. "You saw something, right?"

"I just guessed."

"*I* saw something," she said. "A couple weeks ago at Miami Shores? Richie's dad slapping him around in the parking lot after the meet. I ducked down behind a car and shouted 'Hey,' and ran away like crazy. Next time I see that I'll call the cops."

All this talk about Richie made me feel anxious, so I said, "I'm going to live with Coach this fall."

"He asked you?"

"Almost."

"Your mom doesn't mind?"

"She says that if I want to go to the Olympics, I've got to start training now."

"Maybe I could live with Coach, too."

"Maybe. But coach has a small house, and a new baby."

"I take up about as much space as a cat," she said. We walked up into the dry sand and sat down. Holding hands, we lightly bumped shoulders.

She smelled of baby lotion. I'd never touched a girl's freckles before, but I imagined that Kim's freckles would feel different. Her red hair was beautiful, and her eyebrows were red, too. Her nose was sunburned and straight and ended in a bump dusted with freckles. Her eyes were a blue so dark they sometimes looked black. I asked if I could kiss her.

"I'll bet you've never kissed a girl."

Sure I have, I said. She looked at me with scorn. Spin the bottle? Seven Minutes of Heaven? I shrugged. I bet no girl's ever kissed you like this, she said. She planted her lips firmly on mine. Don't move your head away so fast, she said.

She took her lucky Winnie–the–Pooh towel off her shoulders and draped it over us. From outside came the crash of waves. We kissed and kissed under her towel, fast, slow, slanted to one side of our noses, then to another, kissed as if we'd just invented kissing. It was the first time I'd kissed a girl with my tongue, or been kissed that way.

She let me touch the freckles on her arms. I felt the baby oil on them, but beyond that nothing felt different. She let me touch her nipples, and then I put my hand between her legs, where her bathing suit felt slithery. I'd never done that before. She went still. I thought I'd better remove my hand, but she reached down and held it against her and began to move her thighs, squeezing my hand against her. I wasn't sure of what I was feeling down there, but I could tell it was what she wanted to do. Finally, she took a sharp breath, then laughed. Her thighs stopped squeezing my hand. She leaned her head against my shoulder. She reached down and began touching me.

A very short time passed. "Wait," I said. "Stop." But it was too late.

"Uh, oh," she said. She giggled and withdrew her hand. "It's gone all over your--"

She pulled the towel off our heads and we looked around. It had grown dark. "Time for a swim," she said. We hurried into the water. The undertow tugged at our feet. The water was warm, and the waves crashed against us, knocking us over. When we reached water over my waist, I took off my Speedo, and I was rinsing it out when a monster wave hit me. I folded and went with it, letting it tumble me over and slam me down onto the sandy bottom. I raised my head in foamy receding water to look for Kim. I couldn't see her. I began calling out her name.

"Bobby!" she called. "Hey, Bobby!"

I turned around. Kim was waving from the shallows behind me.

"Your *bathing* suit."

I wasn't wearing it, and it was no longer in my hand. I sank into the water, calling out that I'd lost my Speedo.

Kim yelled for me to stay exactly where I was. She'd get me another bathing suit.

"Wait!" But she'd scrambled onto the beach. "Just bring me your towel!" I yelled, as she leaned down to pick it up. But she kept running.

It was a velvety, silvery, summer night. A full moon, ripe and clear, was rising. Headlights rushed north and south along A1A. Dark figures sauntered along the beach.

I waited. A lot of time passed. I was feeling anxious. The finals must have begun. The individual medley was one of the last events, so I had time. But not much. I imagined Kim, my replacement Speedo in her hand, knocked down by a car as she tried to cross A1A.

What if Kim's coach wouldn't let her come back? What if Kim decided play a "joke" on me? At some point, sooner than later, bathing suit or no bathing suit, I'd run across to the Casino. I imagined the laughter as I ran by, naked.

Another fear was percolating--the loss of what an older kid had called "vital essences." Every swimmer knew that to jerk off before a race was dumb. By fooling around with Kim, had I ruined my chances of winning?

I tried to lurk in the same spot, but the high flood of onrushing water, sparkling with plankton, pushed me southwards with surprising force.

A slight figure hurried along the water's edge, calling in a high, quavering voice. Kim. I stood and yelled and waved my arms.

Kim rushed into the water, crying, "Bobby! Oh, *Bobby!*" She threw her arms around my neck, saying, "I looked and looked! I thought you were dead. Oh, Bobby, I thought you'd *drowned.*" She wrapped her legs around my waist and pressed her face against my neck and burst into tears. A wave knocked us over and after our heads came to the surface she said, "Oh, Bobby, I thought you'd drowned and it was *all my fault.*"

"Did you find a bathing suit?"

She held it up. She told me she'd stolen it from a kid on her team. How old is he? I said. Ten, she said. I pulled it on. It's tiny, I said. She said, You'll swim faster.

We struggled out of the water, crossed A1A and ran into the Casino. We reached the pool deck just as they were announcing Kim's event, the eleven- and twelve-year-old girls' two hundred yard individual medley. She gave me her lucky towel to hold, trotted over and climbed onto her starting block. She was in lane four. She went into her starting crouch. Rosen fired his pistol.

Coach intercepted me. "Where in Sam Hill have *you* been? Everybody on the team has been looking for you."

"I'm sorry, Coach. I went for a walk and got lost."

"You got *lost?* Bobby, are you serious about being a swimmer?"

"I am."

Coach fingered Kim's towel. "I wasn't born yesterday." He pointed at my bathing suit. "You found that when you were out getting lost?"

"The string broke on my other--"

Coach held up his hand. "You've got a race to win. Are you ready?"

I said, "Is my mother here?"

Coach glanced towards the stands. "I don't know."

"Coach, can I live with you and Barbara?"

"During the school year?"

I nodded.

"I don't think your mother would go for it."

"She says it's okay. I spoke to her this afternoon. She's coming up here tonight to tell you she's for it."

"Wait, wait," he said. "This is too much for me now. You've got to understand that right now *all* my swimmers are important, not just you, Bobby. We'll deal with your situation tomorrow. I'll have to ask Barbara. And we've got the baby. Look, I'm sorry, but I've got to focus on *now*, this next race, Bobby. That's my job."

"Coach, please, if I win this race, *then* can I live with you and Barbara?"

"If you win this race, you'll have my sincere admiration and respect. Now--do you have another bathing suit?"

"No."

"Can you swim in that?"

I nodded.

"Okay. We've only got about a minute to talk." He began talking strategy.

I was faster than Richie in the butterfly and the freestyle, but he usually beat me in the backstroke, and he was a demon-- national age group champion--in the breaststroke. This meant that in the two hundred yard individual medley, I was strong at the beginning and end of the race, but vulnerable in the middle.

"Tonight," Coach said, "you've got to teach Richie right away in the butterfly that he's going to lose this race. So take it out fast, but smooth and relaxed. Richie? That little runt'll be coming after you like the devil wanting to collect a debt. You'll need a good lead on him when you go into the backstroke, 'cause that's when you start into Indian country.

"Now, the backstroke: you've got to swim straight, keep your head aligned, bend those arms at the elbow and push right down the body. You've *got* to be even with him when you go into the breaststroke, because that's Richie's specialty. He's got the hunger, just like you. Don't let him build up a big lead on you in the breaststroke, because I know and you know and Richie Alfers knows that when you boys get to the freestyle and the last fifty yards, if you're anywhere near him, *you will take back that race and show him who's champion.*"

There was a burst of cheering and Kim pulled herself up onto the pool deck. Her coach, Mrs. Carmichael, a chunky, blonde woman in a sleeveless white blouse, madras shorts and flip-flops, hugged her while swimmers and officials stood around applauding. Rosen shook her hand. Kim stared up at him, her mouth open. Then she noticed Coach and me and came over, jumping and capering on the pool deck, "I won," Kim cried. "Oh, I won, I *won.*"

"That's wonderful, little lady, wonderful," Coach said.

But she was smiling at me.

"Superwoman." I handed back her lucky towel.

She buried her face in her towel, then looked at me. "I broke the national record."

"You're amazing, Kim." I meant it.

"You're a gutsy swimmer," Coach said. "Maybe you could wish our friend here in the *tiny* bathing suit good luck in his race."

She reacted as if he'd rebuked her--which he had. Kim's smile disappeared. She drew her towel around her shoulders and said to me in a solemn voice, "Good luck, Bobby."

A whistle blew and Rosen called out, "Finals for the two hundred yards individual medley. Eleven- and twelve-year-old boys up."

"You'd better hustle," Coach said to me. "Or they'll leave without you."

The other boys were standing behind their blocks. The Weimaraner was in lane three, shaking his arms and glancing around with his frozen snarl, while his father talked rapidly, poking him in the chest. His mother had already taken up her position near the finish. I was in lane four, next to Richie.

Mr. Alfers pointed at my Speedo and guffawed. He said, "Hey, Bikini Boy."

Rosen looked over at Mr. Alfers. "Clear the pool deck,"

Mr. Alfers, passing, said, "Girly britches ain't gonna make you swim faster, son."

I climbed onto my starting block. The moon seemed to be drifting closer. Spotlights bathed the stands and pool deck in a cold light. A smell of chlorine rose into the air. Underwater lights shone yellow at regular intervals down the length of the pool.

The Weimaraner was on my left, Billy Cardozo on my right. Cardozo and I wished each other good luck. I wished Richie good luck. He said, "Where'd you get them girlie britches? What are you, anyway, some kind of queer?"

Rosen called out, "Quiet on the pool deck."

"I'm going to beat you, Richie," I said. "And then your papa's going to beat you. Everybody knows that."

There--I'd said it. I'd been carrying the words around with me all day. They didn't help me. The words felt bad in my mouth. I felt a plunging sensation inside my chest, fearful that I'd just ruined my luck.

Richie looked like he was vibrating with anger. I'd never seen him like this. "Go fuck yourself," he said to me. His voice sounded strange.

Rosen called out, "I will disqualify the next boy who talks."

"*Go*, Richie!" Mrs. Alfers called from the bleachers.

"*Fuck* you," Richie said in a low voice.

"Stand down," Rosen said. We got off the starting blocks. Rosen, moving in that rubbery, triple-jointed way of his, came over to where the Weimaraner stood.

"Are you all right, son?"

"Yes, *sir*." Richie's voice was weirdly loud.

Richie's parents came out onto the pool deck. Rosen pointed at them and said, "Go back."

The Alfers remained half on, half off the pool deck.

Rosen said to Richie Alfers, "Son, you've worked long and hard to stand where you're standing now. Do you want to swim in this race?"

Richie sighed and nodded.

"Talking when I'm trying to start the race is against the rules. Do you understand?"

Richie, breathing heavily, his eyes now closed, nodded.

"Good." He patted Richie's shoulder.

At his touch, Richie sagged against his starting block and burst into tears. Rosen dropped his hand in amazement. He turned and motioned for Richie's parents. Mr. Alfers got to Richie first, grabbed his elbow and began shaking it, saying, "C'mon, Richie, cut it out." Richie's mother followed. She moved through the men and put her arms around Richie. He buried his face in her shoulder and sobbed. Mr. Alfers, looking puzzled and uneasy, patted his son on the head. I felt shocked and guilty at what I'd done, but also amazed by my power to shake up Richie Alfers.

Rosen called out, "Five minutes!"

Coach appeared at my side. "Into the pool and swim a couple of laps. Stop staring."

Five minutes later Richie had recovered and we were all back on our blocks. Rosen ordered us to our marks, fired the gun, and the race began.

My Speedo was tight, and I was worried over my "vital essences," so in the first lap I carefully revved up, making sure that fooling around with Kim, or shaking up Richie, hadn't sapped my strength or ruined my luck.

They hadn't, I decided, as I finished the first turn. I felt really good. I was flying high in the water, and during the second lap of the butterfly I charged into the lead. I began the backstroke segment of the race farther ahead of Richie Alfers than ever before.

But Richie began to creep up on me. He stroked closer and closer. My worst nightmare, surely approaching. I couldn't fall behind, or I'd die. I glanced up at the stands and saw my mother. I really saw her. She was standing where Mrs. Alfers usually stood. She'd come after all, and she was cheering. I saw her, lost her and saw her again.

That gave me a real boost, and I began the breaststroke segment ahead of the Weimaraner. That didn't last. For a while, Richie and I swam neck and neck. Then he moved ahead. The breaststroke was "his" stroke. I'd known that he'd probably catch up. Still, I'd hoped I could keep my lead. Now my work was to stay as close as I could to Richie. I'd played this role all summer long, and I hated it. Second place. I kept thinking, Please God, *not in front of my mother.*

I saw the back of Richie's head bobbing up and down, farther and farther away in the lane to my left, and I became aware of how my muscles burned, how I longed for oxygen, how choppy the water was. I hated the breaststroke. I hated the Weimaraner for being so good at it.

He came out of the turn and began the freestyle half a body length in front. But I felt energized leaving the breaststroke and turning to a stroke I loved. I'd win or lose in the next two laps--and now that my mother was here, I had no choice. I couldn't see where she was now, but I knew she was there, watching, cheering me on. I *had* to win. So much depended on it. I had to position myself high on the water, breathe cleanly, pay attention to my stroke: the point of entry of my hands, the pull through the water, the follow-up. I began to take back lost yards. Soon, Richie and I were racing side by side. We went into the turn, flipped, came out side by side. One lap to go.

It was now that I made my decision. It was the last thing I could do. I knew that when I turned my head to breathe, my left shoulder dipped, and I created drag. I'd go faster if I created less drag. So, for the last lap, I stopped breathing.

But the Weimaraner stayed where he was. I couldn't shake off that dark form moving through the water at my side. I've never felt so desperate. The Weimaraner was everything that was bad about my life, everything I hated about myself, everything I wanted to leave behind. I began to swim not to win, but to escape. I went into a kind of frantic overdrive, kicking and stroking with a power I didn't know I had, and still not breathing, while my cheering section went crazy, jumping and waving. I knew my mother was one of them.

I remember finishing the race, and Coach's face leaning

out over the water next to my starting block. He held up one finger and shouted, "Amazing!" But nothing made sense to me. Every muscle burned. I couldn't catch my breath. I saw Richie get out of the water and his mother lead him away. I looked around for my mother.

I couldn't pull myself out of the water. Coach and Rosen had to lift me onto the pool deck. People in the stands and around the pool applauded. I didn't believe they were applauding me. I couldn't stand up. I had no balance and my legs ached. I sat on the deck. A doctor came and checked me and said it was lack of oxygen. He said I'd be okay. They carried me over and lowered me into a kiddies' wading pool and said they'd be back in a minute.

"Coach," I called after him. "Did you see my mother there, next to Mrs. Alfers?"

"Was that her?"

"Tell her I'll be over as soon as I can walk."

"I will, if I see her."

I heard Coach say, "That was some race."

"Thoroughbreds, greyhounds, and kids race their hearts," Rosen said.

I lay in the sun-warmed water of the kiddie pool and stared up at the moon. It seemed so close. I couldn't stop crying. Kim came and sat near me on the pool deck, wrapped in her lucky towel. We didn't talk, but I was glad she was there. My mother, I knew, was up in the stands, waiting for the right moment to come down, when I'd stopped crying. Nearby, in the pool, the thirteen- and fourteen-year-old girls and boys swam their races. Next month I'd be thirteen. I'd be in their age group, and starting all over again.

Asset Management

By
Tim Curtis

The DJ's drum and bass mix blared through twin towers of ragtag industrial speakers set in opposite corners of the fraternity's enormous living area. The Delta Sigs annual Halloween party at K-State, Manhattan, was cooking. The sweaty throng of undergraduate revelers caused steam to billow from the gaping ground-floor windows.

Three beers in, Tobias tapped the girl on the shoulder, and shouted, "So what're you, a butterfly or something?"

The girl turned and yelled, "What?"

Tobias flashed an endearing smile. "You're a butterfly?"

"Chrysiridia rhipheus."

"What?"

"Moth. A Madagascan sunset moth."

Tobias looked her up and down. She was maybe five-eleven. Tobias liked that. At six-three he felt self-conscious with short girls. She wore a black, body sock that flattered her full breasts and cute round butt. A Velcro harness between her shoulder blades bore a pair of brightly patterned, powdery iridescent red, blue and green wings. A headband held her long, brunette hair back, and supported a semi-transparent mask featuring a peculiar proboscis, and two dangly antenna that swung wildly about as she bobbed her head to the music's unrelenting thump, thump, thump. Tobias found the weird looking snout erotic.

"Okay, but I'm still getting a butterfly vibe."

The girl tilted her head back, scrunched her dark, shapely eyebrows, and fluttered her long lashes in dismay. "Haven't you ever seen a moth?"

"Sure, but I've never seen anyone dressed like one."

"Well . . . you've never met me."

Tobias nodded at the mask and shouted, "Doesn't that get in the way when you drink?"

"No. Look." She flipped the mask over her head and smiled. "Here's to ya." She chugged her beer, wiped her mouth with the back of a black, leather-gloved hand, and the moth muzzle dropped in front of her face.

Tobias was impressed, and she was pretty. Sparkling green eyes, high cheekbones, fair complexion, well-proportioned nose, straight white teeth and pouty red lips. Tobias thought it was a face he wouldn't tire gazing at.

"So what are you? A drunk college guy?"

"I *am* a drunk college guy, but . . ." Tobias held up his lobster-clawed hands, almost spilling his beer.

The girl frowned.

"What? You've never seen lobster claws before?"

"In tanks. The lobsters look so sad with those rubber bands on their claws. I think they know they're in a restaurant."

Her earnestness surprised Tobias.

"Don't they get in the way when you pee?"

Wondering how he peed was cool. Tobias turned his left crab hand over. He'd glued the reddish-orange plastic claws onto a pair of mismatched fingerless gloves.

The DJ switched to a classic Frankie Knuckles house groove, the crowded room readjusted its syncopation, and the worn, beer-sticky floor flexed and moaned a muffled groan.

The girl nodded her approval. "Louis Sullivan would be proud."

"Who?"

"Form follows function."

The moth girl smiled as her friend, in a Little Bo Peep getup, pulled her backwards toward the kegs set on the frat house's back porch.

Ambling through the party's costumed, drunk and drugged co-eds, Tobias encountered monsters, vampires, aliens, wings of all shapes, colors and sizes to include two girls who'd come as matching Kotex Maxi, Regular Tru-Fit panty liners with wings. He saw showgirls, gangsters, pimps and whores, one

Obama, two Hillarys and a homemaker in curlers. He high-fived six hairy-chested guys tottering about in spiky-heeled shoes. He passed pointy-eared, fuzzy-tailed and whiskered creatures, a carrot and two Mr. Peanuts. When he noticed a penis barfing on the fraternity's DVD collection, and not far off, a spent, ribbed condom bobbing its reservoir tip to the beat wearing a pair of black and white checkered dress shoes, Tobias decided he was way too sober for his last college Halloween party.

On his way out to the kegs Tobias spotted the moth girl and her girlfriend across the teeming room dancing in front of the thundering speakers. Tobias leaned down, nudged his buddy, Ray Fargo, and asked if he knew her. Ray was sprawled out in a tattered La-Z-Boy rocker wearing a diaper, suckling beer from a giant, pink-nippled, calf-feeding bottle.

"Who?"

Tobias nodded toward the dancing cuties and shouted, "The one with wings."

Ray stood on the chair's arms, scratched his belly, squinted across the sea of bobbing heads, and dropped back onto the soiled cushion. "Butterfly, bee or angel?"

Tobias glanced around. There were no fewer than ten girls with wings of one kind or another in that corner of the room.

"That one there," Tobias pointed, "said she's a moth."

"Moth, butterfly, either way, she's hot. I think she's an art major."

Ray tugged at Tobias's shirtsleeve as he studied the girl.

"Yo, Tob, do me a favor will ya?" Ray held up his bottle. "I don't want to lose my seat."

"You're not trolling tonight?"

"She-it." Ray pointed to the bathroom, and flashed a stupid grin. "Every chick in the place passes this way."

Three hours later Tobias was trashed when he spotted the girl heading for the door.

He yelled from the front porch, "Yo, moth, you can't leave now. It's early." He swayed, stumbled off the porch, and struggled to keep his balance.

Still wearing her mask, the girl turned and teetered on her

long, lean legs. "Lobster paws?"

"You know what I think?"

"What?"

"You look like a giant clitoris—with wings." Tobias wasn't a spontaneous guy, drunk or sober, and was surprised he said that.

Before he could apologize, the girl squealed, spread her arms, danced toward Tobias on her tiptoes, pulled off her headband-moth-mask, antenna and all, threw her arms around Tobias's neck and gave him a soft, lingering kiss on the lips. Dazed, lobster-handed Tobias was about to say something, when Little Bo Peep joined her friend, and they headed across the lawn arm in arm toward the dorms. Without looking back, the girl reached around and waved an iridescent moth wing.

Still wasted, Tobias awoke with the vague notion that his orbit had been altered. Later, when his head cleared it dawned on him why. It was the moth girl's kiss.

Art major? Tobias wasn't even certain where the art department was. He was in a different world. The world he'd been creating for himself since elementary school was singular in focus. He was determined to be the governor of the great state of Kansas, but first he intended to become the youngest person ever to be elected to the Kansas House of Representatives.

By the time Tobias entered K-State, he'd run in and won three student elections. At K-State he'd filled his schedule with social and political science courses, and did volunteer work for the local Republican Party chief. Each campaign had been better organized than the previous one, and thanks in part to Ray Fargo, who could run a good campaign when he wasn't wearing a diaper and sucking beer from a calf's bottle, Tobias was now the class of '08's student president. Tobias was smart and competitive, a natural extrovert with wholesome, Midwestern good looks, a broad, white-toothed smile and a firm handshake.

Tobias wasn't one to lose his head, but the longer it took him to locate the beguiling moth girl, the more infatuated he became. He found her two weeks later in the art department's painting area standing at an easel, head cocked to one side wearing a pair of paint-

stained jeans and a tattered T-shirt that read, *Butterflies Are Overrated.*
The room's large, north facing windows washed sunlight onto her
paint-smeared cheeks and glistened on her hair.

Tobias walked up behind her. "I think I like you better with
wings."

She turned, flashing a captivating smile. "Me too. I miss your
claws."

The politician in him seldom felt socially uncomfortable, and
he'd never had a problem chatting up girls, yet he felt ill at ease. He'd
referenced her costume, but it took him a moment to process her
Halloween allusion. He played it off, nodding at the easel. "What're
you working on?"

Balancing her weight on one foot, she leaned back and
folded her arms. "Have a look and tell me what you think?"

Was she being audacious or coy? For all Tobias knew she'd
painted a close-up view of a Domino's pepperoni pizza, a riot of
color and pattern with no discernible image to ground his pragmatic
mind. Rubbing his chin, he inspected the canvas. "Interesting. What
is it?"

"It's a painting. It doesn't have to be anything other than
that." There was no hint of defensiveness in her voice. She simply
stated a fact that had somehow evaded Tobias.

A consensus builder, Tobias dabbled little in the world of
ambiguity. He put his hands in his jeans pockets and shifted his
weight from foot to foot. "Hmm."

"What's your major?"

"Poly-sci."

"What's your sign?"

"Libra."

"Figures. How much do you know about art?"

"Nothing."

"And it shows. You should never ask, 'What is it?' It's lame,
and representation is so passé."

Tobias wasn't listening. He was busy studying her
mannerisms, like the way she'd put her hands on her hips.
Rather than adding an air of authority to her words, it made her
seem childlike. And the way she cocked her head when she was
grilling him, she seemed more inquisitive than rigorous. She

was quirky, appealing, and seemed to have no need or interest in a world where two plus two equaled four.

After suffering a minute of uneasy silence as she studied her creation, Tobias cleared his throat, and stuck out his hand. "I'm Tobias, Tobias H. Johnson. People call me Toby."

She turned to him, took his hand, and held his gaze. "Nice to meet you, Toby. I'm Ellen."

Was it the way she said, "Toby" or the way she looked at him, like she was genuinely happy to meet him? Tobias couldn't be certain, but she looked every bit a future governor's wife. All she needed was a cause to embrace, nothing too political, nothing that might conflict with future bills or budgets he'd be expected to vote or pass legislation on. He needed to be prudent. Something that benefitted underprivileged kids or nutrition, he wasn't certain. Women's health? No, that was tricky. Once a politician started down that road, they invariably found themselves dealing with a woman's right to choose. He'd think of something.

That Friday after burgers and fries at the Skinny Pig, a popular student hangout, Ellen led Tobias to the graveyard near the north end of campus, and drew him down into the tall, dry, yellowing grass. She was assertive, uninhibited. He discovered a moth tattoo while making love. Moths were essentially night creatures, and like all nocturnal things, Ellen remained a mystery, even naked. Her allure was spellbinding, her scent intoxicating.

After getting dressed, Tobias kissed Ellen's cheek and whispered. "So, what was your painting of?"

Ellen frowned. "Demystifying the piece would ruin it. Didn't your mother ever tell you not to end a sentence with a preposition?"

"She sure did," Tobias smiled, "but I told her that was a rule up with which I would not put."

"Touché."

First the Louis Sullivan reference, and now Winston Churchill? This was fun. He'd always found smart sexy. Tobias did his best Boy Scout's honor gesture. "The painting. I won't tell a soul."

"It was a flame's reflection in a moth's eye."

Caught off guard, Tobias laughed. Ellen slumped. Tobias put his hand on her chin, raised her head, and kissed her soft red lips.

"So, tell me, Tobias H. Johnson, what's the H stand for?"

"Promise not to tell?"

"Promise."

"Hazard."

"Wow."

"My mother's maiden name."

"Is she still—"

"No, she—"

Ellen put her hands over her ears, shook her head and sang la, la . . . la, la . . . la, la, la in a sing-song manner.

For the second time Tobias did something out of character. "How would you like to marry the future governor of Kansas?"

Ellen thought for a moment. "Well . . . I'd have to meet him first, right?"

"Honey, how's the next representative from District 52 look?" Tobias studied his wife's reflection in the Topeka Holiday Inn's mirror. "Ellen? Ellen, are you okay?"

Ellen was lounging on the room's king-size bed.

An hour before sunset, and she'd already drawn the shades. The television, tucked into an armoire facing the bed, was tuned to Dr. Phil. Tobias had insisted that she mute the volume because the nanny was having a hard time getting the baby to take his nap in the adjoining room.

"Ellen—the glass. Don't spill it."

"Right of course. No. Not at all. Whoa."

Tobias watched as the screen cast sinister-looking, bluish-green shadows onto Ellen's thin, pale face. She was wearing the same paint-splattered *Butterflies Are Over Rated* T-shirt she wore two and a half years earlier when Tobias found her standing at her easel. Her hair was uncombed, and she hadn't bothered to throw back the paisley-patterned bedcover, which usually creeped her out. Nor had she kicked off her shoes, unpacked her overnight bag or hung up the dress Ray had a stylist pick out for the campaign's finally rally that evening.

Without glancing in Tobias's direction Ellen said, "Special Agent Nut and Honey," she made an ineffectual swipe with her hand as if saluting, "present and accounted for, Agent $C_6H_4Cl_2$."

When Ellen first began calling Tobias, Agent $C_6H_4Cl_2$, it seemed innocent enough, $C_6H_4Cl_2$ being the active ingredient in mothballs. Ellen became Special Agent Nut & Honey.

Tobias spun around. "How many times have I asked you not to call me that? It makes you sound off kilter. If the press got wind of it, they'd eat me alive, Jesus."

"Okay. Jeez, you can be such a mothball sometimes."

Tobias turned back to the mirror to adjust his tie. "Honey, snap out of it."

"You know I'm always distracted this time of day. *Jeopardy,* America's favorite game show is coming on soon."

Tobias spoke to his image in the mirror, "Oh, sweet Jesus, not that *Jeopardy* crap again, not today of all days."

Soon after the baby was born, Ellen became obsessed with *Jeopardy.* She'd even speculated whether or not Alex Trebek was an alien. Tobias played along; it seemed innocent enough. Trebek acted like one with his Mr. Spock-like personality.

Tobias finished adjusting his tie and turned to face Ellen. "How do I look?"

"Absolutely delish."

"You sure?"

"I'm not kidding, navy blue pinstripe in a wool-cotton blend is my all-time fave, and the orange silk tie looks scrumptious. Very tasty. Don't you dare smoke a cigar wearing that suit; it'll ruin the flavor."

Tobias smiled at their little joke. Ellen was a Madagascan sunset moth. Her species had no interest in clothing.

"Honey, leave it alone, will ya? We don't have time for that nonsense."

Ellen was fooling with the hair on the back of her arm, the one that was just a little thicker, and stiffer than the others.

"Jeez, Agent $C_6H_4Cl_2$, you don't have to go all Orkin Man on me—I wasn't—"

"I'm going down to the ballroom. Make sure everything's ready."

"I'll be down in an hour or so."

"No longer, please. The press will be here at seven. And for God's sake, don't forget to bring the baby."

"Do I have to? I mean it's so unpleasant to be around."

Tobias sat on the edge of the bed rubbing Ellen's leg. "Listen, sweetie, little Toby isn't an *it,* and he's not unpleasant. He's a baby for Christ sake. Okay? Listen, honey, I really need you tonight. Ray says a family picture in tomorrow's paper could make all the difference."

"Can't the nanny—"

"Estelle will be right behind you. Honey, please, can you do this for me? It's really important."

"What's our little N1H1 up to?"

Tobias rolled his eyes. "Sleeping in the other room with Estelle."

"Thank God."

"And please don't refer to the baby as a swine flu virus. I know you're kidding, but no one else will." Tobias feared she wasn't kidding. "After the photo op, Estelle can take little Toby off your hands. Okay? And don't hold him at arm's length. They'll think he went poo."

"Eat, burp, shit, cry, that's it?"

Ray had taken care of everything. The Holiday Inn's midsize ballroom's placid décor had been transformed. The large, ornate, crystal-looking, plastic chandelier that hung from the room's high ceiling still dominated the space, and its lights continued to cast flickering sparkles onto the room's unbiased, off-white walls. The thick, paisley-patterned carpet rendered in pastel colors persisted in lending the room a hushed quality, but thanks to Ray, it now had a cheerful authoritative appearance.

Yards and yards of Republican Party bunting were tacked along the walls, covering the buffet table, and podium that stood near the back of the room. Hundreds of red, white and blue helium balloons with bright curly ribbons dangled overhead. Every nook and cranny featured a smiling Tobias flashing a victorious thumbs-up gesture superimposed over the Kansas State Seal. A profusion of state and national flags in various sizes lined either side of the rectangular room. The room appeared ready to host a kitschy historical pageant or accommodate a patriotic funeral for the smiling, optimistic looking young man featured on the posters.

Tobias checked his watch again. The room had filled with supporters, local civic leaders, wealthy, influential business types, and the press was getting antsy.

Ray stepped to the podium. "If I could have everyone's attention for a moment." The room quieted. "It's my pleasure to introduce District 52's next Republican Representative. Ladies and gentleman, Kansas born, Kansas raised and educated, Tobias H. Johnson."

Applause broke out. Tobias sprang to the mic, shook Ray's hand, and spent fifteen minutes rallying his constituents with well-rehearsed talking points, thanking the crowd time and again for their tireless support. When Tobias was through, Ray reminded everyone to help themselves to refreshments. Tobias mingled with the gathering, shaking hands, and making small talk.

The crowd nudged and shouldered the elderly women, who'd arrived at the buffet-table first, filled their tiny plates with tooth-picked cheese cubes and curlicue fruit slices, and showed no intention of surrendering their positions. The sensibly dry, Robert Mondavi Sauvignon Blanc began to run low, and still no Ellen.

Tobias surveyed the room, and checked his watch. He spotted Ray talking with a group of party leaders. Taking Ray by the arm, Tobias said, "Mind if I steal our illustrious colleague for a moment?"

Out of earshot, Ray said, "I sent somebody upstairs ten minutes ago to see what's taking so goddamn long. One picture of the family, and we're—"

A commotion could be heard coming from the direction of the elevators. All eyes turned. A hush fell over the crowd. A wave of queasiness washed over Tobias when Ellen strolled in wearing her Halloween costume carrying their four-month-old baby over her shoulder like a sack of flour. Her moth mask's anxious antenna probed the air about the toddler's head in dangerously erratic elliptical arcs.

Tobias and Ray exchanged frantic looks. Gasps could be heard. Hands clasped gaping mouths as Ellen sauntered toward Tobias. Security guards rushed forward. Tobias waved them off. Ellen handed little Toby to Tobias, stood on her tiptoes, kissed him on the cheek, and adjusted her wings.

Tobias leaned down intending to whisper something in Ellen's ear, but Ellen beat him to it, pulling him in close by his tie. "Toby, baby, you have no idea how exhausting lunar navigation can be. I feel like I've been—"

Cameras flashed, whispers and awkward laughter filled the ballroom as people began to realize the costumed woman was their candidate's wife. Ellen turned to the crowd, lifted her mask, smiled and waved. Applause broke out. Ellen fluttered her wings, curtsied, and began to wander about the room greeting people and shaking hands.

Tobias stepped to the microphone. "Happy Halloween everyone, our son's first, and my wife's favorite holiday. Thanks for all your support, and don't forget to vote this Tuesday."

Tobias circled the room patting little Toby on the back. People cooed at the baby. Tobias and Ellen converged in the center of the room.

"I've got to be out of here in ten," the photographer from the *Topeka Capital* said. "If I could just ask you to stand here, and if your wife could look up . . . yeah, like that. I'll tell ya, for a minute there I didn't know what to think."

The camera flashed, and Ray had his All-American, aspiring politician, happy family image for the morning newspaper. Estelle appeared and took the baby from Tobias.

Ellen turned to follow Estelle, but Tobias caught her by the hand, pulled her close and whispered in her ear, "Honey, we need to make another doctor's appointment."

"Right, of course. No. Not at all. Whoa. I hope you're not too upset. You wouldn't believe Trebek tonight. The Apollo 11 moon landing and all that? Well, I don't have to tell you—you know I'm mad about the moon."

Ellen gave Tobias a peck on the cheek, and scurried off to catch up with Estelle and the baby before the elevator doors closed.

After shaking another hundred hands, kissing powdered cheeks and enduring more hearty pats on the back, the gathering wound down. By eight thirty-five Tobias and Ray had settled into the back booth of the hotel's bar.

Ray tapped out one last text, and put his cell phone down. "Jesus Christ. I can't believe she pulled that moth shit. Scared the hell out of me. But you handled it, man." Ray held his shot glass up, tossed his drink back, and wiped his mouth with the palm of his hand. "You were smooth, pal. I spoke with the press and the party reps. We're going to be okay."

"I'm out."

Ray slammed his glass on the table. Three guys wearing ball caps sitting at the bar swung their stools around, and checked out Tobias and Ray before turning back to the TV over the bar tuned to NFL highlights.

Ray leaned in, giving Tobias a hard look. "I'm out? What the fuck does that mean?"

"You saw Ellen. She's not right."

"Listen, asshole, we're in this together. No fucking way I'm going to let you bail on me four days before the goddamn election."

"I'm sorry, but—"

"Four more days, that's all I'm asking. We've got a real shot at pulling this out. Then we can spin it anyway you want."

Once Ellen learned from the Little White Wedding Chapel's webpage that they had presided over the marriages of Frank Sinatra, Judy Garland, Mickey Rooney, Paul Newman and Joanne Woodward, Michael Jordan, Bruce Willis and Demi Moore, Britney Spears and Patty Duke—twice her mind was set. Except even the low-end #1 Tribute to Elvis Wedding Package, performed in a pink Cadillac in the chapel's Beautiful Tunnel of Vows Drive-Thru, cost three-hundred-twenty-five dollars. That included Elvis singing romantic love songs before and after the ceremony, but even so . . .

Tobias and Ellen agreed to wing it. Just the phrase *Sin City* whispered by either of them, caused them to drop everything, and seek an illicit location where they would make love. They had done it many times in Tobias's '04 Jeep Wrangler, in the shower down the hall from Ellen's dorm room, under the gym's bleachers, in a

Macy's changing room in Topeka and once in the alley behind the Skinny Pig.

The bloated, middle-aged Elvis impersonator, justice-of-the-peace, and used car salesman of the month at Budner and Sons Quality Used Cars and Trucks pulled a flask from his hip pocket, took a swig, wiped his mouth on the sleeve of his unbuttoned-to-the-fly, high-collared, yellowed arm-pitted, sequined jumpsuit and belched before saying, "You may now kiss your little sweetie pie."

An intense ray of Las Vegas sunlight ricocheted off Elvis's spangled collar, momentarily blinding Tobias. The dry, super-heated, desert sunbeam seemed to bore a narrow hole into his brain. Through blurry eyes he saw a beautiful, mysterious butterfly standing before him. For the briefest of moments, Tobias felt he was free falling, and wondered if he'd made a terrible mistake. As his head cleared, the butterfly morphed into an image of Ellen wearing her Halloween mask.

Ellen swept the mask up, and put her hand on Tobias's cheek. "Toby. Toby, baby, are you okay?"

The New Beginnings Matrimonial Chapel and House of Deepest Contemplation was a block off Las Vegas Boulevard, under the Stratosphere's shadow, tucked between the doublewide trailer that functioned as the Budner and Sons' office, and the heavy-duty plastic covered structure that housed Alvin Budner Junior's Custom Auto Detailing Shop and American Indian Gift Emporium. The tiny chapel featured the patch of well-worn Astroturf on which Tobias and Ellen were standing, a small, ornate three-tiered plastic waterfall surrounded by ten dusty, fading, potted plastic palm trees, and smelled of cigarette butts, wet dog, Chinese carryout masked by Elvis' musky scent and Jamaican ganja.

Tobias blinked and saw Ellen gazing up at him with a look of alarm in her eyes. She looked like a frightened little girl trying to cross a busy street, and in that instant Tobias fell under Ellen's spell once again. Tobias smiled and kissed his unpredictable, vulnerable young bride.

"Listen, pal, I'm in a bit of a hurry. I'm this close to closing," Elvis held up his yellowed, nicotine-stained thumb and index finger to indicate a quarter-of-an-inch, "a deal on that red '09 Hummer over there." Elvis nodded toward the front of the car lot.

Tobias winked at Ellen when Elvis said *hummer*. Stifling a laugh, Ellen traced a moist arc along her upper lip with her tongue.

"So if you could initial here and here, and sign at the bottom."

Elvis handed Tobias an official-looking document with the seal of Nevada on it secured to a clipboard by a set of spring-loaded false teeth. "Same goes for you, ma'am." Elvis patted his drooping black pompadour. "You-all owe me a hundred and fifty bucks. You got cash, right?"

Tobias initialed and signed where indicated, handed the clipboard to Ellen and reached into the front pocket of his wrinkled slacks, pulled out a roll of twenties, peeled off eight of them. "You got a five and five ones?"

Elvis frowned. "Love Me Tender," was included, "Viva Las Vegas," wasn't. Twenty-five percent gratuity is recommended."

Tobias shrugged. "Keep the change."

In a Southern drawl, Elvis said, "Thank you very much." He turned, held his practiced Elvis pose for a second, and barged through the chapel's beaded-curtained doorway. Tobias and Ellen watched as Elvis headed toward two guys giving the Humvee the once over the way construction workers admire pretty girls.

Tobias made the dean's list his last semester at K-State. Ellen graduated cum laude. Three weeks later they hopped into Tobias's Jeep, and took off for Las Vegas camping along the way. Tobias and Ellen caught the Bellagio Resort and Casino's awesome water display from the sidewalk before heading back to Topeka via the Grand Canyon. They made fevered love in their sleeping bags at night with the Southwest's majestic vistas sprawling out in front of them and whenever they were overtaken by the sheer joy of being married.

They'd rented an apartment in Southwest Topeka. Tobias worked for a Washington lobbyist. Ellen sold art supplies part-time at the Hobby Lobby Creative Center on Wanamaker Road, and painted in her dining room studio. Tobias drifted off to sleep listening to Ellen recounting their wacky wedding or rambled on about the Madagascan sunset moth. She said it was vulnerable because it was a day flying creature with a lunar personality. Its bright colors were meant to warn predators of its toxicity.

Tobias wasn't certain what a lunar personality was, but comparisons weren't hard to come by. Ellen was a day person, and preferred bright colors. She was impulsive and undeniably vulnerable. Ellen bestowed moth kisses with her eyelashes.

Six months later, Tobias began his run for Southwest Topeka's District 52 with Ray Fargo as campaign manager. They were both ambitious, and the local Republican Party caucus took notice.

Ellen the asset Tobias assumed she'd be, at his side for photo shoots, and fund raising events. People found her distant yet warm, a little flighty in a good way, charmingly candid, and genuinely happy to meet them.

Five months into the campaign Ellen became pregnant, quit her job and spent much of her time alone at home. By her second trimester, Ellen had become withdrawn and stopped painting altogether. Her presence on the campaign trail became less frequent and her gaffes more so.

"'I fuck my husband?' Jesus Christ, Toby, put a fucking muzzle on her if you have to."

"It was kind of funny."

"Sure, if you were running a fucking Kool-Aid stand, but it could tank the campaign if she pulled that crap in front of the wrong people. It took me six goddamn phone calls over two days to convince Conner to keep a lid on it. Thank god he represents the trucker's union. You really think the League of Women Voters would find that shit funny? Or the district's school board?"

"I get it. I'll have a talk with her."

"Great, and while you two are having your little chitchat, ask her to stop playing with the candles in restaurants, and staring at the flame like a goddamn idiot."

Tobias sat back and studied Ray. "You can be a real asshole sometimes. You know damn well Ellen's not a fucking idiot. It's the pregnancy that's making her spacy."

"Listen, Toby, I like Ellen, always have, but it's not just your career on the line here. You go down, I go down. It's too late to jump ship."

Tobias hoped he hadn't grown so accustomed to Ellen's quirkiness he'd missed something.

Curled up in Tobias's lap, Ellen played it off. "Ray's paranoid. It was calculated, trucker talk. Fidget with a candle, and space out once in a while, big deal. Pregnancy's like being strapped into the front car of a hormonal roller coaster taking banked turns at full speed." Ellen put Tobias' hand on her stomach. "I'm trying to be supportive, but I get bored listening to you and Ray go on about taxes and spending, Medicaid, Medicare, farm subsidies and education. It's all so reactionary."

Ray was blowing things out of proportion. Mental health problem? Tobias didn't think so. And besides, he'd fallen in love with Ellen's eccentricities. Tobias felt the baby kick, leaned down, smelled Ellen's hair, and kissed the top of her head. He chalked it up to the pregnancy, and tried to not think about the time he'd given Ellen a massage.

"I love it when you type code on my spine."

Ellen gave birth four months before the election. When her postpartum blues didn't subside after a couple of weeks, Tobias made a phone call, told the doctor that Ellen's personality had gone flat, she hadn't been eating, wasn't sleeping, and showed little interest in the baby. The doctor said it sounded more serious than the usual postpartum blues. Ellen stopped breastfeeding the day before their appointment.

"First of all, I look and feel like shit. I'm sensitive to light"—Ellen affected a laugh—"and have developed a fondness for fine fabrics. Big deal. But a postpartum condition? No way."

Tobias took the baby and gave him his bottle when he began to fuss. "She says her clothes itch, she keeps the shades drawn and wears sunglasses around the house."

Ellen shrugged. "Diurnal, nocturnal, can't a lady change her mind?"

Tobias looked at Ellen. "Babe, please."

The doctor looked concerned. "Is there something I should be aware of?"

Ellen rolled her eyes. "It was a joke."

The doctor checked Ellen's chart. "Have you heard of postpartum psychosis?"

"What is it with men? First I squeeze a nine pound slug through my birth canal, my hormones take me on a carnival ride, and suddenly I'm a psycho?"

"I'll start you on a conventional antipsychotic so you can go back to breast feeding if you choose to. But you have to promise you'll take them. Otherwise there's a very good chance you'll need to be admitted. Now . . . you may experience dry mouth, muscle stiffness, muscle cramping, tremors and weight gain."

"That sounds pleasant. I can't wait."

The next day, Ellen said, "Well, thank god," when Tobias hired a nanny.

Ellen was preoccupied with that damn hair again. She spent hours testing that defiant, protruding stubble, drawing her fingertip over it, gauging its springiness, feeling its vibration subside, searching the surrounding area for other wayward bristles. When she first noticed it a few months earlier, Tobias joked, said it was a fly hair, maybe a whisker, nothing to worry about. But she wouldn't let it go . . . and now—an antenna through which Trebek gave her orders? That was no laughing matter.

She said that if she strummed it just so, Trebek's clues came in loud and clear—decoded. When Trebek stated, "With 301 miles, it has the most coastline of current states that were part of the 13 original states," Ellen said the 301 was an encrypted phrase alluding to the moon's effect on the tides and 13 signified the thirteen lunar cycles.

"Ellen. The nanny? Her name's Estelle. She has a lot of experience."

"With psychos?"

Tobias and Ray sat in an IHOP booth on Southwest Topeka Boulevard. A week before the election they were behind in the polls. Despite all Ray's efforts, the other candidates were getting on the evening news more often, selling their positions with well-phrased sound bites.

Ray studied the raindrops gathering on the glass, while he and Tobias waited for their coffee. Ray dumped four spoonfuls of sugar in his cup and stirred it a long while. "I can't believe I'm saying this, but we need Ellen and the baby at Friday's fund-raiser. It's our only chance to pull this out."

"Shit. Ellen's been—"

"Listen, these goddamn rumors are sticking to us like flies on shit."

"Are you suggesting we go public with Ellen's—?"

"Hell, no. We're in Kansas, Toto, remember? Even if our constituents were ready to embrace a frank discussion about postpartum depression or worse, they're not ready to vote for a candidate with a loony wife. Maybe after the election, but not now."

Tobias resented the loony bit, but he knew Ray was right. Tobias hated the idea of losing, but the thought of a victory at Ellen's expense made him queasy.

Tobias grew impatient waiting for the elevators, and climbed the three flights up to their room. His was clammy and weary legged by the time he tossed his coat and tie on the room's wingback chair. Ellen stood at the bathroom's mirror wearing her butterfly pajamas. In the harsh light she looked as weary and drawn as Tobias felt. Their eyes met in the mirror. Tobias slipped his arm around Ellen's waist, and kissed the top of her head. She closed her eyes, leaned her head back on Tobias's chest. They rocked side to side, Ellen patting Tobias' arm before removing her makeup. In the adjoining room Estelle sat on the edge of the bed filing her nails. Little Toby didn't wake up when Tobias kissed his baby's puffy cheeks.

Tobias had been pacing St. Francis Hospital's seventh floor hallway for an hour when his cell phone rang. The sun was just coming up.

"Ray."

"I took care of everything."

"Yeah, I saw the paper already. Thanks."

The morning edition featured a picture of Tobias looking into the camera holding their grinning baby, Ellen wearing her winged costume beamed up at Tobias. The caption stated, "Citing Personal Issues, Candidate Johnson Abruptly Quits Race."

"I spoke to my guys and a few bloggers. Follow-up stories should focus on postpartum depression, earlier detection, warning signs, where to get help . . . that kind of stuff."

Tobias stared at his reflection in the windows next to the elevators overlooking the parking lot. He looked old for twenty-five. "Sorry about this."

"Forget it, I'll be okay. How's Ellen doing?"

"She's sedated. The doctor said this was the best thing that could have happened."

"Funny guy."

"He said gone untreated she and the baby would have been at risk. Better now, before something really bad happened. They're going to treat her symptoms, and when she's stabilized do a complete mental evaluation. I told him everything including the moth stuff and *Jeopardy*."

"*Jeopardy?*"

"I'll you about it later."

"So, what happened?"

"Woke up around one-fifteen. Ellen's crouched in the corner, tears running down her cheeks, chewing . . ." Tobias's voice broke, "on my goddamn tie." He took a deep breath and collected himself. "She'd ripped the suit up too . . . the medics never found the coat pocket . . . thought she might have swallowed it."

"Jesus Christ, that's hardcore."

"No shit. It freaked me out." The elevator opened and an orderly stepped off wheeling an empty gurney.

"I'm really sorry." The line was silent for a while. "So, what're you going to do?"

"Make sure Ellen gets the treatment she needs. My boss said with the right spin, this could become the next cause célèbre within the healthcare debate—and the party would look good taking a proactive stance."

"So you could still land on your feet."

"That's the last thing on my mind. All I want is another chance for Ellen and me to—"

"To what? To grow old together? Jesus, Toby, don't go all

sappy on me. Shit, now I've got an image of you and Ellen starring in a Cialis commercial."

"I'm not being sappy. I'm just saying—"

"Just because Ellen went a little wacko doesn't mean—"

Tobias held his phone to his mouth and raised his voice. "Christ, Ray, do you have to be so goddamn insensitive?" A nurse walked by putting her finger to her lips.

Tobias nodded and put the phone back to his ear and heard, ". . . Stuart, you know . . . when life hands you lemons—"

"I can't even believe you have the balls to quote Martha Stuart at a time like—"

"Listen, Toby. Don't do anything you'll regret later. You'll get over this. If this postpartum thing takes off, Ellen's little flameout could be an asset."

"Ray, I'm not—"

"Okay, okay. I'm just saying let's not burn any bridges. In two years we could be sitting pretty. Hell, you could be the next—"

Tobias touched the disconnect icon on his cell phone's screen, and rested his brow on the cool plate-glass window. Day break had arrived, and he watched with jaded eyes as the faint circles of illumination surrounding the light poles in the parking lot went dark one by one like candles being blown out on a birthday cake.

Meet the Authors

Michael Creeden — *Fervor*

Michael Creeden was born in Fall River, Massachusetts. After graduating from Southeastern Massachusetts University, he worked for fifteen years as a technical writer in the software and biotech industries. He began attending Friday Night Writers in 2005, when he was a student in the Florida International University MFA program. He has been a semi-regular attendee since then, coming for inspiration, camaraderie, and the quality feedback that John and the group provide. His short stories and non-fiction have appeared in *Miami Living*, *The Florida Book Review*, and *Tigertail*. He lives in Miami, where he teaches writing at Florida International University.

Ingrid López – *Semper Fi*

Ingrid wrote her first tragedy at age seven on a Soviet typewriter she says was "roughly the size of a family sedan." She soon discovered that writing was the perfect loophole for lying without getting in trouble. "As long as I typed it up and called it 'fiction' my mother never threatened to break out the dreaded *Chancleta*—that's a flip-flop for those of you uninitiated in the art of Cuban child-rearing. It is a truth universally acknowledged that all Cuban children quiver and pale at the mere mention of *The Chancleta*."

Ingrid has been a member of Friday Night Writers for about four years. "There's nothing like a captive audience to improve the craft," she says. "It's nice to bask in the warmth of glowing reviews by your best friend and your dog, but ultimately, constructive criticism is the only way to get better at anything. With the exception of skydiving.

Louis K. Lowy – *A Hole in the Night*

A former firefighter, Louis K. Lowy is the author of D*ie Laughing*, a humorously dark sci-fi novel set in the 1950's of flying saucers, communist paranoia, and live television. He is the recipient of a State of Florida Individual Artist Fellowship. His work has appeared in, among others, *Coral Living Magazine*, *New Plains Review*, *Pushing Out the Boat*, *The MacGuffin Magazine*, and *The Chaffey Review*. His poem "Poetry Workshop" was the second place winner of Winning Writers Wergle Flomp Humor Poetry Contest. He can be reached at www.louisklowy.com and on Facebook.

Louis has been involved with Friday Night Writers for six years. He originally joined as a means to connect with other writers—not really sure what it was, exactly, that connect meant. Over the years he's come to realize that it means an opportunity to learn from its leader, John Dufresne; a safe ground to be criticized and praised; a forum to share in the insecurities and triumphs that come with writing; and a network of friendship, support, and encouragement.

Lizabeth Solomon – *Lucky*

Before moving to South Florida from Chicago in 1993, Lizabeth planted the first seeds of a novel on paper. In 2001, having left her job, she dedicated herself to trying to finish that book. After sending perhaps the fifth (or fiftieth) revision to her longtime friend and editor for a read-thru, her friend replied by sending a book from the slush pile at work: *Love Warps the Mind a Little*. It's really good, and in the author's notes, he thanks this writers group." Lizabeth has been a devoted member of John Dufresne's Friday Night Writers since.

Lucky grew from an observation while shopping at the Publix at Hollywood Circle (Florida), though the story takes place in Chicago. If not an active participant of the Friday Night Writers, Lizabeth doubts that *Lucky* ever would have been more than a passing pondering or unfinished rendering, attesting that the telling of this tale was both inspired and improved by the writings and feedback of her peers.

Lizabeth has written articles for a handful of Chicago and South Florida local publications as well as the *Chicago Tribune* and its syndicate. This is her first published short story.

David Beaty – *Swimming Against the Weimaraner*

 David Beaty has lived and worked in Greece, England and Brazil. A graduate of Columbia College, he earned an MFA in Creative Writing from Florida International University, where he was a recipient of the Josephine Friedman Award For Fiction. His stories have appeared in *Miami Noir, Unbound Press, Having A Wonderful Time, Tigertail*, and other anthologies and literary journals. His short story, "Ghosts," was chosen for The Best American Mystery Stories 2000, and his story, *The Last of Lord Jitters,* received honorable mention in *The Best American Mystery Stories 2007.*

Tim Curtis – *Asset Management*

Tim Curtis wrote his first complete sentence seven years ago. He was so excited he immediately signed up for evening classes at Miami-Dade College. Two years later he joined John Dufresne's Friday Night Writers group. Thanks to spell check, and the feedback he received from the group, Tim was accepted into Florida International University's Creative Writing Program the following year. This fall marks his sixth year attending Friday Night Writers and his fourth year in FIU's three year MFA program.

When Tim isn't busy rewriting his awesome comedic novel Live Is Good—If But Briefly, he dabbles in short stories and poetry. Tim never shies away from a chance to share his writing, and is available for bedside readings from his tome of early missives he modestly refers to as "sedative literature."

The Last Word

John Dufresne's Friday Night Writers meets on selected Friday's during the academic school year on the campus of Florida International University, Miami. Writers distribute thirty copies of their work to one another at each session. The work is limited to one chapter, or short story, at a time. All submissions are typed in Times Roman, 12 point, double spaced, with one inch margins. For current information check the group's website at http://www.fridaynightwriters.com.

www.ingramcontent.com/pod-product-compliance
Lightning Source LLC
Chambersburg PA
CBHW020916180626
46816CB00007BA/2434